North of Jesus' Beans

short stories
by

Bill Gaston

Cormorant Books

Published with the assistance of the Canada Council,
the Ontario Arts Council, and the Ministry of Culture
and Communications of the Government of Ontario.

The author wishes to acknowledge the support of the
Canada Council.

Previous versions of these stories have appeared in the
following magazines: "The Summing of the Parts",
"The Work-in-Progress"—*Canadian Fiction Magazine*;
"The Walk", "Lying Lights"—*Exile*; "Big Animals", "North of
Jesus' Beans"—*The New Quarterly*; "Heaven on Earth"—*Matrix*;
"The Green House"—*The Fiddlehead*; and "Why the Retarded
Are Here on Earth"—*The Shambhala Sun*.

Also by Bill Gaston: *Deep Cove Stories, Tall Lives,
The Cameraman,* and *Inviting Blindness* (poems).

Cover from a colour transfer, enamel, etc., on paper entitled
Problem, by J.W. Stewart, from the collection of the Canada
Council Art Bank, courtesy of the artist.

Author's photo by Bev Thornton.

Printed and bound in Canada.

Published by Cormorant Books Inc.
RR 1, Dunvegan, Ontario, Canada K0C 1J0

Canadian Cataloguing in Publication Data

Gaston, Bill, 1953 -
    North of Jesus' beans : short stories

ISBN 0-920953-57-3

    I. Title.

PS8563 . A76N67 1993   C813' .54   C93-090421-4
PR9199 . 3 . G38N67 1993

CONTENTS

For Vaughn Thomas

NORTH OF JESUS' BEANS

The alarm, the croaking buzz. Mark whispered low in her ear. Donna grunted back. Mark lurched up on an elbow. A winter morning, it was still dark.

"Scud alert all clear." He slapped the switch down.

"Did you have to say that?" said Donna.

They could hear rush hour outside, and winter wind. One thing about working in the same office was they couldn't both phone in sick. Not that they'd get in trouble, not with their seniority, but they'd be ribbed. Sudden flu, right. In her raucous stage whisper the whole floor could hear, Jo Beck would ask them what they did on their sick day and how many times did they do it.

Donna and Mark didn't want to take the day off for sex, or a hangover. Ironically, they hadn't done such a thing since years ago, when it was indeed risky at work. This morning they were tired from staying up two nights watching the Gulf War.

"My soul is tired," said Donna, in the bathroom. She was peeing; he was shaving. "It feels attacked."

"I dunno yet," Mark said. "So far it looks okay. Quick and painless maybe. Maybe they'll just surrender."

"It's a massacre," said Donna. "It's revenge. They think the world is with them and they're going crazy."

They showered together, a habit from more playful days. Now, like a brick in the toilet tank, it was practical, responsible: one lathered while one rinsed, and so the planet would be saved. This morning it was cold to be out of the warm stream, and a few times they more or less elbowed each other for it, though they weren't aware of this.

"The precision stuff seems to be working." Mark talked loud over the spray. "I mean, Baghdad looks perfectly safe."

"You're amazing. It's their station and it's their war and you're ready to believe what they edit for you."

It was clear the war would be fought at home too. Not that Mark was in favour of the war. It was a question of stance, of how outraged one should feel and for what reasons. One's skill at sifting either side's propaganda. Mark made a mistake suggesting some of her anger stemmed from embarrassment that her kid sister had married a guy in the Canadian army. He was a bombardier-something, and according to Donna's sister Judy he was "dying to go to the Gulf." Instead, he'd gotten leave and they were visiting this weekend. It would be hell.

In the car, Donna watched Mark's wet head steam in the cold. After the twenty-minute trip to work his hair would be dry. One of his little jokes was, I don't dry my hair, I drive it.

Donna drove, Mark searched the radio for news. At a stoplight they heard that eighty-six percent of Americans agreed with their president's action in the Gulf.

"I find that hard to believe," Mark said. "How can so many people be so stupid. Sanctions were in place. Or they could have just killed Hussein. It's like they're actually glad there's a war." He shook his head in wonder. "I mean, there are lots of regular folks down there."

"I wonder what Ariel thinks?" Donna said softly.

"Ariel!" Mark paused and thought. "Ariel. Jeez."

The name had not come up in years. Mark and Donna

looked at each other, then back to the traffic. But their eyes were inward with memories.

After a minute Donna ruined it by saying, "I don't think there's any question what Ariel thinks."

* * *

California's magic had to do with the sun, but not just because it shone day after day. It was more the quality of light. In it appropriate colours were born. Pastel blue, washed green, and faded red, a pink even men looked good in. The bone hue of Hindu cotton looked a proper part of the landscape. Tibetan rainbow vests suggested the mystical wonder hiding behind this California light, the power fleeting and untouchable except at certain times or on certain drugs at certain places. It couldn't be talked about, but it always was.

Mark and Donna arrived at Big Sur from Ottawa in the spring of 1970. Their Valiant was dubbed Princess, cute humour with a twist. A friend had spray-painted crude Canadian flags on both doors. It was otherwise rusted out, and full of camping stuff and books and clothes, so they couldn't pick up hitchhikers. So many hitchhikers! People who looked just like them. And who smiled even while being passed.

It felt like they were coming home. So many people just like them, in gas stations, cafés, sometimes just sitting beside the road, stoned or whatever, in no hurry, which of course was the point. Feeling corny at first, Mark and Donna returned the peace signs flashed by people who looked in some cases sincere and philosophical, in other cases like misfits who saw in this hippie world a chance to fit in. Some were extroverted, a few obnoxious. Mark and Donna felt a bit humbled by the courage of Americans, who seemed to be embarrassed about absolutely nothing.

They were told Big Beach had gotten weird recently, but they went for a look. The surf was up and mist blew through pockets of people like its aim was to cool and cleanse. Donna saw dark looks traded here and there, and she pointed this out to Mark, who was gazing around with a smile that wouldn't quit. They almost bumped into a man in a loincloth babbling to himself in true lunatic fashion. They saw an older guy, forty maybe, masturbating in the logs, watching a pack of nude women running after a frisbee. On the way back to the car they were accosted for money by a girl who looked twelve, who had ice-blue eyes that went into her head forever.

But it was all quite wonderful. They had arrived.

Little Beach was harder to get to, which was why it was still perfect. They hiked in, saw, and immediately hiked back for their stuff. They'd seen families, naked except for red bandanas, toeing about in tidal pools. They'd seen a bonfire and a circle of men playing guitars. On the way up to the car a pixie-ish guy sitting on an aimless rock shared a joint with them. He had a black flute in his belt. He said little, just grinned a lot, and of course there was no question of money.

Carrying their tent, searching the high-tide jumble of logs for a place to make their home, Mark and Donna were stopped by a classic hippie in full beard, and robe of rawhide and feathers. They would later learn he was The Name Man, and this would be the only time he would talk to them. Multicoloured beads were braided deep in his beard.

"What, man, be thy name?" he asked Mark. The Name Man's arms were up like Merlin's. His eyes were a mix of grand seriousness and quirk.

"Uh, Mark."

"Uh-mark. I have not heard tell of Uh-mark. Is Uh-mark thy true name?"

"Mark."

The Name Man hesitated just two seconds. "Mark: thou wearest the mark of Cain. Pursued. With wit, thou stayest free. Mark: the sign, the seal, the rune. Mark: the examination, the grading, the fail, the pass, the judgement."

The Name Man stared at Mark like judgement.

"Welcome to the beach." He dropped an arm and motioned with a flick of his head that Mark should pass. The Name Man's beard rattled. Mark walked by. The Name Man turned to Donna, arms up.

"What, woman, be thy name?"

"Does this mean," Donna smiled, "parents have foresight?"

"Parents?" The Name Man was stung. But he quickly recovered. "Ward and June? Foresight? No. No more than dice. 'Tis a wondrous web, the synchronicity, time and space and wave and nibbits of sand, thine progenitors be conduits of missing linkage, and every name by the nature of naming can not and never be an accident."

"Oh."

Donna found out that she was both the Virgin and the Mother. A womb of lambs and blood. She was both lust and innocence.

"Firstly and foremostly," said The Name Man, slowing down, arms labouring at waist level, "thou art beauty, thou art great good looks, and it hast nothing to do with thy face."

* * *

The interior of ORS (Office of Regulatory Services) was done in colours meant to offend no eye. It was hard to say exactly what the colour was, off-grey or pale brown or even a green. Donna called it gov-grey, a colour no one was supposed to notice. Which was government's function too if it ran well, she said.

It bothered Mark that she considered the business of government to be a scramble to avoid offending anyone. He thought this a cynical view of democracy, let alone their careers.

It was obvious from the faces on the ORS floor that everyone had suffered two late nights watching the war. Jim Peters, their immediate superior, left his glass cubicle, looked at his watch and did the buzzer joke. Jim Peters did this once a month or so. He'd watch his watch and count, "Five, four, three, two, one," then make a buzzer noise. He did this whether they were early or late, and he did it to show that he could mock the punch-clock mentality. In fact, Jim Peters was the only one in the office concerned with time, or people being late.

There was another joke. At ORS they shuffled so much paper they had to laugh at it from time to time. How many trees did you kill today, etc. Lore had it that any sheet of paper could not be folded more than six times (Mark tried it, it was true.) The joke declared that ORS people were hired because they could fold paper seven times, that is, they were good at bureaucracy. Jim Peters, Mr. Bureaucracy himself, joked he could fold paper nine times.

"Remember," Jim Peters would say after giving Mark or Donna advice, or an order, "I'm a nine."

* * *

After five weeks on Small Beach, Mark and Donna went inland. It was a hard move. They had made lifelong friends, reached heights of joy and tranquillity. Sex had been good, and sometimes they walked a ways into the forest and did it standing up, having discovered they shared a thrill-fear of being seen. Mark learned nine guitar chords and had written his own song. Donna had been shown Tai Chi and did it each dawn at water's edge, naked. Mark loved to wake up and roll over and watch his love, a small figure down there in the mist, seeking body's truth.

But because of the mist nothing was ever dry. A loner named Tim down the beach had his traveller's cheques ripped off from his tent in broad daylight. Lately, straights in long pants had been striding the beach, ogling the bare-naked hippie girls. Donna went back to wearing her bikini bottoms. Mark gave gawkers a shame-on-you stare. They either stared back or ignored him. Or shrugged and smiled, blameless. Americans were so different.

They packed their Valiant and ten miles in stopped at a gas station converted into a café. The new owner was up a ladder, painting the new sign. They were to find out his name was Ariel. He was darkly Jewish, with an Afro and heavy New York accent that at first sounded stupid to them but later not. The sign's background was sky blue, the letters canary yellow edged in crimson. It read: Jesus' Beans. Above this name was a grinning, wiseass, cartoon Jesus.

* * *

In her slot Donna found a packet from the adoption agency. The next stage, it said, was a series of visits to an adviser, who'd "assess their probability of success." This really meant, Donna had heard, that they'd be raked over the coals in order to prove them unsuitable. Donna understood. They doled out babies, and there were not enough to go around. She herself doled out money, and the more people she could discover were undeserving, the fewer she had to feel bad about for not giving to.

Damn, was it ever odd how back and forth she went on this adoption thing. She stared at the new forms and wondered if she should even bother. It was like applying for a promotion she probably wouldn't get and wasn't even sure she wanted.

A baby, god. Donna had no doubts how overwhelming it would be. She wondered if Mark really knew this. How even an adopted baby would roar into their lives, the flesh and blood and shit reality exploding a conceptualized notion of Baby as quickly as—a smart bomb killed a desert bunker.

But Mark was eager. He'd joke, pointing at the three songbirds in their cage, yelling, "Birds are not enough!"

So why was she doing most of the work? Donna imagined herself walking the forms over to him saying, You're so eager, you do it. Because here she was doing shitty paper work, doing the diapers already. Though Mark would be horrified to know her thoughts. He always insisted he'd do half. Last week he'd made Jim Peters assure them that some sort of job sharing was possible.

She stared at the forms, the paper grainier than it used to be, the recycle logo at the bottom. Recycled baby. Huge wonderful icon that she was supposedly incomplete without.

Donna wondered if any Iraqi babies would become available. Middle Eastern. She liked the word Persian. A Persian baby. Honey-coloured skin. Almond eyes. Accusing eyes.

* * *

They would do dishes, wait on tables and, Ariel explained,

"just common sense help around." In return they got a room, all the food they wanted and, Ariel said, "maybe some money if there's enough."

The first day, the three of them washed walls and drank tea, selling nothing more than candy bars and soda and giving directions to beaches. Ariel got a ladder to do the ceiling, and from up there he explained angels to them. "Angels," he said, "are what won't let something stay the same. Angels shake things up." He said this with a smile, but also with utter certainty in his eyes. It was difficult not believing Ariel when he talked like this. "Sometimes it feels like they're messing things up, sometimes they beat the shit out of you, right? Only the long haul will tell if it was an angel or not." Ariel had an afterthought, laughed. "Once an angel came to me in the form of gonorrhoea."

He had his shirt off. Both biceps had blue tattoos, the kind you gave each other in prison. Ariel told them an angel had given him this gas station. Donna asked him what he meant.

"Just that," said Ariel.

"Well, how do you know?"

"I know." He smiled. It was impossible to disbelieve him.

"Did the angel know he was an angel?"

"She. No. Angels are not often self-conscious."

* * *

The worst part for Mark was seeing the Scuds fall on Israel. The reporters in that TV station hearing the explosions and getting into their masks, the look on their faces. Mark felt sick to his stomach. What would Israel do? They had nukes. The world's chain of hate went so far. Israel uses nukes, Russia withdraws from the coalition; Egypt and Syria turn their tanks around; Muslim Pakistan has nukes too, declares war on Israel. Here we go.

Mark sat silently, watching, wondering if this was in fact the end of the world. He said nothing to Donna, who was upset enough. He'd never forgotten hearing, way back when, maybe in California, that Cayce, Nostradamus, the Bible and other places too predicted global apocalypse in the decade they were now in. Though not a believer in anything, Mark had never quite dismissed this titbit. Why had all the seers, unknown to each other, picked this decade out of infinite others? What the hell.

Donna passed the potato chips. Neither had eaten. She had adoption forms on her lap, about which they'd been talking during commercials. When the Israeli thing started, they just watched. Mark took some chips and said thanks like it was a normal night in Ottawa. Pretending he wasn't horrified to the core, he bit one delicately as the sirens wailed over Tel Aviv.

* * *

Jesus' Beans became a hangout, in some cases a refuge from beach life. Ariel's blackboard menu was vegi-Mex, mostly bean and rice and cheese concoctions, but he had burgers in the freezer for anyone who asked. In winter he ate some meat himself, he told Donna.

A few people complained about the sign, saying it belittled the Saviour. Ariel conducted a loose poll. Atheists thought it a great sign. Of Christians, half thought it was good to proclaim Jesus as a revolutionary. Some loved depicting Christ's sense of humour. Of course there was no way to question Christians so offended by the sign they hadn't come in at all.

Mark and Donna liked it there. Ariel was a perfect

host. He let penniless wanderers camp out back. He fed them and was gentle in urging, after a few days, that they get on with their lives.

Ariel seemed older, wiser, in some moods charismatic. Maybe New York City made you that way, Mark and Donna wondered. After a month Ariel partnered up with Maria, a severe Honduran who looked all of thirty-five. She too seemed wise, but had little humour. She rolled her eyes at Ariel for giving Mark and Donna a hundred dollars one week, and the next week asking them sheepishly, but with a big ironic smile, if he could borrow fifty back.

Together Ariel and Maria seemed wiser still. They helped people through bad drugs, no money, psychic freefall, abandonment by lovers. At times Ariel's smiling touch was the key, sometimes Maria's stern advice. On weekends beach folks would come up for a bonfire. Guitars, singing, wine, smoke. Wit, wild ideas, laughs. More laughter than tears by a long shot.

It really was magic. After one bonfire Donna and Mark and Ariel and Maria and a guy named Ray took off their clothes. How it began was unclear. Mark and Donna, unsure where this was heading, signalled wariness to each other with their eyes. Maria saw them and smiled. Mark eased the tension when he said, People from Ottawa don't get naked very much.

But it wasn't like that. They lay in the grass, putting their heads together, forming a five-pointed star. Ray was an astronomer. He told them about light-years, celestial energy and neutrinos passing through their bodies even as he spoke. At one point someone started to laugh, and then they were all laughing, five heads touching, and Donna could feel in her skull the resonating bone of four other heads. Five-toned laughter, a wild yet harmonious joy, rushed out of control for ten, twenty, who knew how many minutes—time held five selves in a shocking, spinning, loving grip. It was the best Donna had felt in her life.

* * *

There's little to recommend Ottawa in the winter, except perhaps skating on the canal. It is acceptably eccentric to skate to work and some do, bent like Hans Brinker, briefcase tucked to the chest, scarf flying behind. That was the idea, anyway.

Mark and Donna didn't live near the canal. They had no skates in any case. Today they drove home quickly, agreeing to postpone shopping-day. They discussed an odd notion that in watching the war they were somehow aiding and abetting it. They decided that was incorrect. It was important that they watch it, in the sense that it was important to know the enemy.

Mark ordered pizza. Donna fed the birds. She hardly noticed the birds now except when she fed them. This is when they sang loudest. They were called Medicine Birds, three males, purple with yellow beaks. When people asked Mark why they were called Medicine Birds, Mark looked at them like they were stupid and joked, "Because they're purple."

The pizza came and they sat. The trick was to zap to and from CNN and the CBC channel to see who had the breaking story. Live Pentagon briefings were shown on both, but the CBC carried more global opinion, or news of anti-U.S. riots. Last night an Iranian official had described a scenario whereby, if certain coalition governments fell due to swelling anti-U.S. rage, you had the makings for a Third World War.

Mark grabbed some pizza, and the zapper. He looked at Donna and said, "Planet Earth, the Movie." He zapped.

The CNN logo appeared, a drum-dirge, then a commercial.

Sometimes Donna hated his flippancy. Sometimes he tried too hard to be funny. He wasn't funny when you could see him trying.

Speaking of trying too hard, Brian Mulroney came on. In that awful anal whisper of his he parroted George Bush's words. Donna was mad that Canada had missed the chance to perform enlightened politics.

After watching a debate as to whether Scuds could contain chemicals, Donna asked Mark to turn it off. She needed a break, she said. Mark didn't move. She repeated herself, adding a firm "please". Mark hit the off button. The TV clicked and faded. Staring at it, Mark said, "Warrus interruptus."

In the new silence, they could sense each other's minds.

"Maybe," Donna said after a long minute, "we shouldn't bring a child up in this kind of world."

"That's a stupid thing to say," Mark said. He threw a crust into the box and reached for another slice.

"Why is that a stupid thing to say?"

"Because the kid's already here. Somewhere. Or will be. Some kid will get a better life if we adopt it. It's simple." Mark looked at her. "You were spouting a cliché birth-parents use. You didn't think."

Mark was right, of course. That is, she'd said it wrong. But he was being a prick. She'd actually meant something else. She didn't bother trying to explain. She asked for a piece of pizza and he passed her the whole box. They both faced the blank TV. What she'd wanted to say wasn't exactly clear to her. It had to do with her wondering whether she had any love left for a baby. Or whether there was any love left in this cold fucking city, or in this cold fucking world. Or whether—this was it—or whether there ever had been love here at all.

* * *

They knew they were living in a golden age. Around the fire people sometimes talked of this, and Mark could feel it, feel it swell in his chest and throat. Sometimes Ariel would talk of spiritual love and Mark could hear that Ariel's throat was thick with it too. Sometimes Mark felt he could almost weep for joy. In the magic California night, he could sense vibrant colours around them, and a benevolent spirit overhead and underneath.

They would never forget people they met. One woman, "a pal of John Lilly's," she claimed, had done early dolphin work with him and had just last month dropped acid in one of his isolation tanks. She wasn't very likeable but, lord, the stories she had! And they met a rich guy who had just bought an old circus cannon and was trailoring it down to the beach, did they wanna come and watch? Watch what, Mark asked. See for yourself, the guy winked. Reportedly the police stopped him later and took it away, along with a stash of challenging drugs.

They met a guru-type with immense eyes, and a converted bus housing four women. A practising polygamist! Ariel called him Henry the IV. Donna argued with him, and soon the man was going on like some Iron Age Bible-thumper right out of the desert. They met another guy, six-six with a hook nose, who claimed he was born joined to his brother at the big toe. At the fire he gulped wine and showed a bulb of toe scar. He got drunk and a bit mean, took out a ukulele and shouted twisted spontaneous poems.

There were angels all around, the disruptive kind one had to learn to like. A dope bust on the beach made

everyone wary. A murder at Big Beach, though no one
except wire-heads went there any more. Then Ariel was
busted for selling beer, and had to close Jesus' Beans down.
He opened up as a private dwelling, "sharing" his food with
whoever came by, accepting "donations" according to the
Xerox price list Ariel and Mark and Donna kept handy in
their pockets.

Donna and Mark's own angel arrived after Maria and
Ariel fought and Maria left for parts unknown. It was a wet
spell, not much beach traffic. Business was down. While
not exactly mopey, Ariel was quieter, sipping beer by
himself, mid-morning. He slouched. He smiled from time
to time to assure them he was okay.

The café looked shabby of late, as if reflecting Ariel's
spirit. He'd let supplies run low, and sometimes they ran
out of essentials like cumin or tortilla flour. The sign had
weathered too. A rock had removed an eyebrow, making
Jesus look more criminal than mischievous, and the crimson paint that bordered the yellow letters hadn't adhered
and was coming off in strips, hanging like crêpe after a
violent party.

Mark was edgy. He didn't want to lose this life or this
job, such as it was, but for some reason time felt ripe. Some
hazy line had been crossed, some new season entered. But
he and Donna agreed they should stay as long as needed.

Mark suggested Ariel fix up the place, maybe adver-
tise more. Maybe a sign right out there on the highway. Or
one a mile up the road, saying, "Last Chance Beans Till
Japan."

Ariel smiled a tired version of his smile. But he said
no.

"This place is just part of the landscape. It's a natural
thing. Maybe it gets all worn down and ugly, or maybe it
doesn't. People come, or not. That's the way it is."

Ariel stretched lazily, a crackling in his shoulders. Because of that smile, Mark wasn't sure how serious he was being.

"I mean, folks throwing rocks at a sign is an environmental thing. Like hail. Folks come in or they drive by. Either way it's okay. It's a huge weave. I'm just a part of the weave. I don't believe in forcing things."

Donna tried cheering him up. While Mark swept and scrubbed and whatnot, she sat across from Ariel, bringing up this and that favourite topic. But Mark could tell that Donna was like water off a duck. She was thinking she was uplifting him, and Ariel was just being polite. Ariel was always at least polite.

But his eyes did fire up again, when he learned he and Donna shared the same birthday. Ariel was six years older to the day. Donna and Ariel agreed that of course astrology was superstition. But—they laughed hugely—in their case it was true! For they did have the same take on things. In any case it was fun to speculate on the stars and fate and, as Ariel kept calling it, the weave. By afternoon Ariel was a bit drunk, and Donna had her three-beer buzz on. They decided to go for a walk and smoke a joint.

Watching the two of them talk and laugh, first about how Maria made love, and then about stuff Donna liked to do, had made Mark a bit nervous. He was nervous again watching Donna and Ariel leave holding hands. Of course Mark was being stupid. If they were up to something would they hold hands in front of him? Ariel touched anyone who looked open to it. Once he had even sort of caressed the back of Mark's neck. It was in front of customers and hadn't been sexual at all. After a few seconds of shock, Mark got off the little joke Americans seemed to like. "Hey," he said, "I'm from Ottawa."

Donna and Ariel were gone an hour. Mark served a

straight-looking couple with matching love beads: academics researching hippies, or goofs from the 'burbs out to live dangerously, or narcs. Though in the end they proved to be quite nice. Gentle. Canadian, almost.

Donna and Ariel returned. Ariel came to Mark, looked at him significantly and said, "I'll be in my room, man." Then slouched away.

Now Donna was looking up at him. She looked more surprised than sad. She touched his wrist.

"We just...," she began. "Jesus, Mark. Ariel and I just made love."

She was shaking her head as if in amazement. She looked near tears, but she was also smiling. As if to say it was all—even me and you, standing here like this in pain— it was all part of a weave, an amazing weave.

* * *

"Be nice to them," Mark said.

"Tell me why I should be nice to them," said Donna, her back to him, hands in suds, careful of knives.

In the current argument, Mark proposed it would do no good to be hostile to her kid sister and her soldier-boy. He argued that peace began on the home front—simply by being compassionate to all. It was a humble beginning, but the only beginning, for peace on a global scale. Donna listened patiently.

"I don't," said Donna, "recall everyone smiling and being all friendly and then *nicing* down the Berlin Wall."

"I didn't say nice, I said compassionate."

"You said we should be 'nice' to Judy and Roy."

"Well don't mock my argument just because I get a bit lazy with words."

"Well how do I know what the argument is except by

the words you use?"

It wasn't as if they were bickering more lately. They were just agreeing less. They'd talked about this too. And they had decided that it was as though, after twenty years, they were both too tired to be other than bluntly honest with each other.

Donna washed and Mark dried. Donna came up with a way to sum up her side of things.

"Every barbarian you can make ashamed of his lust for war," she said, "means one less barbarian who'll pick up a gun."

"I think shamed barbarians are the most dangerous. The most violent," Mark countered.

"I didn't say shamed. I said *ashamed*. Jesus!" She raised her voice because Mark was leaving the room. "To be ashamed suggests self-understanding."

Mark called back.

"So what if all the barbarians on one side get ashamed and quit? Won't the other side just invade?"

Donna had to sit on a stool and close her eyes. She yelled slowly and clearly. "Now you are talking about something utterly different!"

"I am! That's right! I agree!" Mark was laughing, but not maliciously. "We agree at last!"

* * *

Mark's angel took ten more years to arrive and he didn't share it with Donna. Perhaps one reason he didn't share it was because the angel's name was Pru. There were other reasons. She was embarrassingly young, and tiny-bodied, making her look younger. She was a temp at ORS. Mark could picture Donna's reaction, could see her hard smile and hear her say, "PROOO?" She would see it as a typical mid-life thing. She would not listen to him describe Pru for what she was. Pru was extremely complex.

Though what wasn't complex? Not even sex was simple any more. With Donna it was still enjoyable, but he had to crank it up a bit. Sometimes in the middle of it he found himself thinking inappropriate things, as in a crass comedy: the office, what inning the Jays were in, what he should make for dinner.

Pru offered good old senseless lust. Sure, youth if you like. Then Pru had gotten complicated too. The affair lapsed into a casualness. Sex began to feel . . . sensible. And Pru began to make minor demands, began to get careless in her eye contact at work. Mark discovered he was terrified Donna might find out. Because, Jesus, it might actually break them up. After this many years. Life without Donna? What would that be like? Could it be a good thing? Did he want to risk finding out?

He began to conjure explanations he might use. The one he settled on (but never had to resort to, for Pru broke it off) was that something dark and unforgiving in him wanted to pay her back for Ariel.

Which may or may not have been true. Mark recalled how the worst emotions had run their course quickly—the burning rage, the shame. How he had reconciled with Ariel before he had with Donna. How Ariel had bent his mind by knocking on his door and explaining calmly, "You don't feel bad because of what Donna and I did. You feel bad because of jealousy."

The nerve of the bastard. Pokes your girlfriend and lectures you on feelings. But what Ariel said made sense. Turning him in on himself had given him the tool to fix his pain.

The next day, Donna looking sheepish, or ashamed—in any case she avoided both of them—Mark and Ariel threw a frisbee out back, sharing a bottle of bourbon, laughing about how everyone thought they were so smart but always acted like dumb animals in the end. Ariel told Mark about the time he let himself be seduced by his father's girlfriend. Though humbled by the big-city-ness of Ariel's story, Mark shared his tale about being fourteen and putting a rock through Sheila McKee's bedroom window.

A week later they said goodbye to Ariel and other friends, oiled up Princess Valiant, packed food and counted out gas money. They started north.

It was sad. In fact, leaving Jesus' Beans shoved reconciliation on a back burner. Leaving showed them that, so rich had their stay been, the thing between Ariel and Donna was but one event in a huge Event. Ottawa was going to be grey. But they would return to California.

The reconciliation—the real talking—waited until Montana. Mark yelled and Donna cried. Donna yelled and Mark tried to cry. Mark told her he felt like a wimpy feeb for being too civilized, or afraid, to attack Ariel on the spot. He didn't tell her he feared she thought him a wimpy feeb too, at least subconsciously, and always would.

They agreed that human beings were by nature non-monogamous. But that the pain of non-monogamy outweighed its pleasure. They agreed—after Mark declared he felt no need to get even—to be monogamous together, for life. Donna punctuated the agreement with a little joke, saying, "How very Ottawa of us to be able to talk like this."

Thus formally engaged, they drove several rosy-glow miles in silence. Mark told a joke too. He was allowed to be cynical for he was the one who'd been wronged. It was a dynamic that was to persist. Mark looked across the gulf of dreadful stability that had arisen between him and Donna, and he asked, smiling, "We gonna name the kids Wally and The Beaver?"

* * *

Mark hoped Donna's motherly concern for her sister would keep her from being testy with the soldier-boy. Mark was bloody tired of the war, and talking about it. If it came to an argument he would grunt agreement with whoever was loudest. It was obvious nobody knew anything for certain, not Bush, not Hussein, not Donna. Maybe the only one who knew something for certain was an Iraqi peasant cowering under a bush as a jet screamed by.

Mark was stirring his special Stroganoff and Donna vacuuming when the buzzer rang. How long it had been ringing was anybody's guess, because as soon as Donna turned the vacuum off there it was. Before opening the door to them, Donna said something about the military being exactly on time.

Judy was taller than Roy. Roy was a surprise all around. He was extremely handsome except for his glasses and a big butt. And his height. But he had the face of a model. In the way he said hello and shook hands Donna saw traces of macho and nerd both, a strange mix. Judy laughed at everything Roy said, so as to clue them in to Roy's dry humour. Roy was bright, that was clear from the start. There would be no jokes at Roy's expense.

They began to eat. No one said anything for a minute.

"You don't know," Roy announced, shaking his head over his loaded fork, "what deprivation can do for the taste buds. This is wonderful."

Roy, Judy informed them, was being transferred to New Brunswick. Unless he went to the Gulf, which wasn't likely.

"Sending us grubs over," Roy interrupted, "would indicate a major policy change by Mr. Mulroo. Ain't gonna happen."

It was the first mention of the war. Mark watched Donna eat, staring at her plate.

"But if it's policy, it'd be Mr. George doing the changing, wouldn't you say, Roy?" Mark asked. "Not Mr. Mulroo?"

Roy's eyes brightened.

"That's exactly right. Mr. George owns the war, no doubt about that one. It's their turkey-shoot. Everyone else it's just good politics."

Donna kept looking at her plate.

The rest of the meal they discussed a life in New Brunswick versus Ontario, then they crammed into the kitchen to talk and do dishes. Roy eased a thin cigarette out of his pocket.

"Who'd like to smoke a joint?"

"Roy," Judy exclaimed, "that's rude."

"It's okay," Mark said. "Fire it up."

It had been years since Mark and Donna last smoked. Nothing like a decision had been made; it was more a case of fewer parties, changing friends. Donna surprised herself by shaking her head "no" as Roy passed the joint to her.

But the smell was nostalgic. Donna stayed quiet and watched. It looked strong. Mark got tongue-tied and nervous and tackled the dishes. Judy began to giggle. Roy was humming and drumming his fingers on his knees. Donna suggested the three of them relax in the living room while she finished up in here.

"So, wanna check out the war?" she heard Mark ask Roy in the hall. That polite, subservient tone of his annoyed her.

"Hell no," said Roy. "Aren't you sick of that yet?"

Mark laughed. "I just thought it was sort of your sport, so to speak."

"Hey," Roy laughed too. "I'm on vacation. Gimme

a break."

When Donna joined them, Roy had on his lap an empty canvas bag stencilled with white numbers. Mark was struggling with odd metal goggles. He got the straps right and slipped them on. The eyepieces protruded two inches, like tiny telescopes, and looked extremely goofy. Judy turned and saw Mark for the first time and shrieked with laughter. Roy started belly-laughing. So did Mark, though he couldn't see himself.

"I know a game," Roy said, catching his breath, putting his hands up to stop everyone's laughter. The glasses, he explained, let you see in the dark. It was fun if you turned out the lights. The one wearing the glasses was "God", and told everyone else where to walk.

"And if God feels like it, God walks you into a wall," Roy said, smiling like a nerd, shrugging.

"No, I know!" Mark yelled, suddenly child-like. He went to the birdcage and opened it. He lifted one of the Medicine Birds out and tossed it lightly into the air. It lit on a curtain rod across the room. One other bird skipped across the cage floor and followed the first, landing by its side.

"We'll hunt birds!" Mark said. He turned to Roy and Judy. He didn't look at Donna. "They won't move in the dark. They sort of go to sleep. We'll hunt them blind. God can give directions."

Donna had decided to go to the bedroom with a book when Mark turned to give her the goggles. He was smiling hopefully.

"You first."

The goggles were surprisingly heavy, made of thick metal and painted olive green. The straps were stiff, bulky canvas. On the front was a dial that clicked when you turned it.

"Forget that thing," Roy told her. "The adjustment's broken. That's how I got them. You can keep them, by the way. Little present from Mr. George's army."

Judy began in the kitchen, flicking out all the lights. Donna figured the straps out and pulled the goggles on. The last light went out.

Magic. Everything was tinged greeny, or red. Most everything was greeny. Red things, Donna determined, were bodies, people. That's what it was, heat. The colour almost seemed a sound, a droning. Everything was vibrant, crackling almost, like aurora borealis. Things broken down to atoms, dancing. It was beautiful. There was her little sister, a flame she could almost hear, feeling her way along the wall back into the living room.

Donna realized she had been moaning aloud.

"Not bad, eh?" chuckled Roy.

Its power lay in the fact that it was real, Donna decided. Real but not normally seen.

"I know where one bird is." Mark's voice.

Donna turned in the direction of her husband.

There he was. The lines of his body were so familiar. But between the lines he was a buzzing crimson. He seemed to glow more brightly red than the other two. How could that be?

Mark was holding an arm up. He pointed a finger like a gun. On it perched the third Medicine Bird. Mark was leaning forward, straining to see the bird. He couldn't. Donna could see him smiling in his trying. Mark looked new and wonderful. His teeth were the wildest colour she had ever seen.

LYING LIGHTS

—Beausejour, Manitoba, 1934

When Lise the Métis housekeeper talked of the future she smiled. Her eyes, fixed on John's shirt, and wide, did not seem to know the smile was there.

"When you grow up," Lise announced, perhaps in some secret spot, like the pocket of a dry drainage ditch, "you will travel some place far from Beau, farther away than Winnipeg, and find a girl."

"How do you know?" John asked, as always forgetting to plan for the impatience this question always brought.

"Because that's what *happens*," she shouted, stamping her foot like an English girl.

Beausejour abutted the main railway and had seasonal farm work, and so saw its fair share of bums. Only a handful ever got jobs, and the town saw to it that the rest moved on: it was the one time when Beausejour boys were allowed to throw rocks.

Old Bert Flute somehow managed to stay near town for five summers running. He rarely ventured into town itself, and as far as anyone knew he didn't steal laundry or garden crops. Some supposed he had a woman on the reserve. ("But we know that's not true," Lise told John, declaring in her whisper that they knew Bert Flute best.)

It happened that their secret spots were Bert Flute's as well: under trestles or in dry ditches, Bert Flute would unfurl his bedroll, make a tripod and fire for his spaghetti pot, and say to himself, "Home." When John first met him, Bert Flute had a shelter made out of old sandbags below the flood-bank of the Brokenhead River. The riverbank was a bazaar of paper and muddy trash, a mile of spring flood jetsam caught on twigs. The air hung rich with the shit-smell of river mud, and as Bert Flute greeted them that first time, Lise whispered to John, "I think that man's been pooping near here."

He was a small man, bald, with a pinched yellow face, and though it was May and almost hot he wore a long "bum's coat", the sleeves hanging down so far they hid his hands. He stood before them and bowed low, and then stuck out his left hand to be shook.

"Most pleased, most pleased. Bert Flute, my tads, Bert Flute," he chirped in a high, singing accent as he took their hands in turn. He smiled so squeezed and wrinkly a smile John couldn't tell if he was joyful or wretched. He watched for tears.

After such an elegant introduction all three of them fell silent. An old bum, a Métis woman, a staring boy. Bert Flute saw Lise's wrinkled sneer as she sniffed the dank air.

"Eh? Spring-time, eh?" He jerked his head up and looked about quickly, sniffing too. "Weddin' time! Water, mud, weeds, wheat—ol' damn earth fulla *fock!*" He shot his small fist into the air, and laughed. When Bert Flute moved it was always out of stillness—then a quick, exaggerated jerk, like a startled prairie dog.

"Fulla *fock!*" he yelled again, and again up went the quick fist. Then he went still and stared at Lise's young sugar-beet breasts.

"*You* know well the spring, eh, my miss?" he said, staring, and before Lise had time to shout or slap, his left hand reached out, brushed her breast and produced a penny. With no break in movement he turned and gave the cent to John.

Bert Flute's sleight-of-hand kept John in awe and Lise smiling over summer days to come, as did his one-handed cats-cradles made of muddy river string, his crudely carved birds and his funny, spring-time voice. But what struck John the most was what blazed behind the man's quickness, and what mesmerized even when he was still. It blazed— like half-hidden, hissing colours—mostly in his face, especially when he shouted or cried, and he did both often. He spoke of his "fightin' friends", and laughed; he shouted about civilization, then cried; he laughed about "you beauteous children", then went still, and tears started. John could see that whatever it was that made Bert Flute cry was also what made him laugh. He reminded John of a jackrabbit he'd seen whose side got torn under a plough.

It had to do with his chicken hand.

Bert Flute always kept his right hand well hidden up his sleeve, and didn't show John or Lise the hand until August of that first summer. He was telling them another of his stories, a long one. Today the story concerned a "fresh tad" from the old country who came to the U.S. of A., then Mexico, Vancouver, then Winnipeg; was refused jobs, laughed at by children, screamed at by "flowerin' girls". The man moved on, "saw men die and gov'ments burn", worked at odd jobs, but always in back rooms or at night. All of this because of "a wee problem".

"A wee problem," Bert Flute whispered, eyeing John and Lise hard and going still, nearing a ghost-story surprise.

"A wee problem," he said again. "For the man—were his poor mum accursed by toads? were his dad's own tool off-centre?—for the man came into this wide world . . . *draggin' this!*" He punched his right hand out of its sleeve. Shrunken. Pale blue, gnarled claws, the nails black, cracked, overlong. A chicken-hand.

Bert Flute held it out in front of them, squeezed up his face and laughed wildly. And then cried just as hard, his inner blaze shifting only in colour, not in heat.

Once that first summer, John's slowness with things made him ask for a better look. Lise shushed him, but the old man smiled, seeing that John lived in a world where people talked too quickly, loved for hidden reasons and played jokes, so he calmly produced the hand and let John prod it and pull the fingers, which fell limp when he let them go.

"No, it can't move for me," Bert Flute whispered, and as John continued to play, the man's face darkened and tears started.

"Can you write, lad?" he asked softly. John nodded. "I be fifty-two, and not one letter from these fingers. My folks," he spat now, "would not have a left-handed boy, would not add strange onto strange. . . . *Fifty-two!*" He began to cry in earnest then, flinging his head back for full-throated donkey-brays.

Another time they arrived at Bert Flute's home—two blankets hung on nails under a creek bridge—to see him off downstream, standing rigidly with feet apart, screaming and flapping his chicken-hand at something distant—maybe at fields and trees, or maybe at bright cities, with their flowerin' girls and bosses.

Exactly what John learned from Bert Flute is not clear. Perhaps, compared to the stoic farmers and their silly children, of all people John had yet met, the hobo showed him best the shaggy span of emotions humans were bedevilled by. Perhaps Bert Flute was best at revealing John's own stupidity to him. Bert Flute was so different from his parents or anyone else in Beausejour, and yet, next to Lise, he seemed to understand John the most.

That first summer Bert Flute told them how he'd "learnt himself flyin'."

"It's like this," he said, slit-eyed and sly as when he told all stories. "First you pretend a bit, boy. Can you pretend?" Lise nodded yes, he could pretend. (John wasn't so sure.)

"Pretend that your eyes be at the horizon, be stretched out there, hangin' onto land's end with little eyeball-claws. . . ."

"Horizontal," said Lise to John, giving the sign with a finger. She always translated this way for him, and whenever Bert Flute grew more whimsical, Lise got more scientific.

"So," the man continued, "the eyes be as a blanket to cover the whole prairie." He pretended to smooth down a blanket that led out from his eyes. "With eyesight so, your nose pretends to be as a tree, standin' there in front of your head."

"Vertical," explained Lise.

"You now have the crosshairs of a rifle!" Bert Flute was excited, and punched the air. "You're pretendin', mind you, but you *got* crosshairs whatever they say." Bert Flute studied Lise and John, who stared at the horizon, aiming with their noses.

"Crosshairs. Rifle," he repeated. "Now, what do you shoot? Great bullets?" John and Lise said nothing.

"No! you shoot . . . your*self*! It's a *brain*ride!" He screeched triumphantly. "You fly, you fly far, over the farms and trees, out into a cosy hot spot in the air, you zither like a dragonfly out there in midcentre-point!"

John tried to shoot himself and fly, but failed, as he always failed with imagination. But he did remember something of his past, and spoke up.

"When I was small. I never really flew as a dragonfly,

but I could look far. Way off over all the snow. And not think."

The old man looked at John curiously, and after a moment said, "Yes, yes. And not think. You be givin' old Flute a lesson, boy. 'Not think'—that should be step one to my tellin' of flyin'."

"When I was younger," John added, "not so much now."

"That's all he could do, is stare," Lise said, nodding.

Bert Flute often performed his penny-from-Lise's-breast trick for them, and John never tired of it. And each time it happened, he saw how Lise did a kind of trick herself. A double-trick: she'd look nervous, and little-girl shy, and yet as soon as he touched her she took control of everything, of Bert Flute himself, by acting stiff and queenly as a pretty grade-twelver when asked to the harvest dance by a scared farm boy. Odd how, whenever the old man touched her, Lise could become a pretty woman, and as if by magic turn Bert Flute into a silly boy who always removed his hand. John thought this a marvellous trick. When he asked Lise how she did it (walking home one day after Bert Flute had tried to touch both her breasts at once), she just shushed him, and told him not to tell anybody anything, or they'd all be in trouble.

John was fourteen and Lise nineteen when, while on one of their winter walks, Lise's own teachings took a sudden turn. Perhaps it was innocent, perhaps not. But John, at least, hadn't expected it.

A Sunday walk in early March. The night's wind had moulded drifts, some six feet deep, under the eaves of houses and against barn walls. With snow so deep, secret spots were hard to find. So John and Lise would make their own: tunnelling into the larger drifts, they discovered what

Eskimos knew, that snow houses are warm enough to take off a coat and sit in. And more.

It took fifteen minutes to dig an eight-foot tunnel, and another ten to hollow out a "bedroom". Then they'd glove away enough ceiling to allow some light in through a foot-thick snow roof. They'd be sweating from the work.

On this Sunday their bedroom was smaller and warmer than usual. They had tunnelled hard to get here, laughing as they went, dog-digging snow in each other's faces. They rested now, still flushed réd with fun. All that linked them with the outside world was a soft yellow ceiling glow which made the room seem more secret than usual, as if the snow lens over their heads allowed only the softest part of the sun.

They'd finished lunch, were propped back to back, and Lise talked. Once more, about love. This time, to John's amazement, she was casually painting a word-picture of how "He" would look. She seemed certain of his hawk-like nose, his green eyes, blond hair and one crooked tooth. He would be tall and slim, without much hair on his body. Lise paused at this point, and stared up to the lemon-lit ceiling. John tried for something good to say.

"I have thirteen pubic hairs now," he said suddenly, in a tone almost apologetic, as if he had too much hair for her, "and my dinger, I think, is almost a man's."

"So!" she said, and giggled, "let me see them!"

The bedroom was just high enough for John to kneel in front of her. He undid his fasteners, and moved his pants and underwear down to where his knees met the snow, in shadows. John began to count.

"One, two, three . . . there's a small one . . . four . . . five, six. . . ."

"Let me," said Lise. She crouched lower, her face a foot away from his bare groin; she pushed his hands away.

"Okay. Seven, eight . . . nine, ten, eleven . . . there's twelve . . . there's thirteen. And there's fourteen. And another small one . . . fifteen."

"Some must have grown."

Lise shushed him. "I think I feel some more here," she said, "on your *testes.*" She began to smooth her hands over his testicles, which had been high and hard, but now they softened in the warmth of Lise's cupped hands and eased down slowly. John felt his penis go hard.

"There," he whispered quickly, "there. That's what happens in the morning. Look . . . ," he said, and pointed past her face at his erection. Lise laughed softly.

"Don't you ever think about girls?" she asked, her voice breaking, and deepening.

"Well . . . no. Yes: I think about you, and Mother. . . ."

Lise interrupted.

"This is what lovers do," she whispered, and then, extending her tongue, but keeping the point of it soft, she smoothed it along and around John's scant pubic hair.

The light which barely brought out colour on Lise's check-shirted back began to pulsate with John's own heart-beat. He could feel Lise's tongue more and more as, strangely, his eyes and ears and thoughts themselves moved down to sit and swell in his stomach, and then in his groin. His body seemed huge, all parts magnified.

"This feels strange . . . hot," he said, his voice a whis-per now too, a whisper that stood out and shook in the smooth light of their bedroom.

"This tickles my tongue," she whispered back.

"Your tongue . . . feels like . . . a very polite dog," John said, which made Lise groan, and then bark softly, and then laugh like a child.

II

John could not fathom Lise's affections. Her body, yes, he enjoyed that. In secret spots, her bedroom, the hockey shack, anywhere. The act of lovemaking amazed him—a wonder and colour that hummed in his body, a body that, each time it tried, knew how to find pleasure in itself. But lately Lise had been confusing things, spoiling things. With her talk.

His father caught them once in her bedroom. John would often answer her soft, middle-of-the-night knock and follow her across the hall. After sex, when Lise began to sleep, a vision of his parents' faces would always help John make his dutiful way back to his own room. But on this particular night Lise didn't want him to stop. When she finally did, John was exhausted. The cold room and howling mid-winter wind, mixed with Lise's embrace and soft breathing, kept John from seeing the faces, or his duty. He fell asleep. In the morning he barely heard his father's brusque pounding on his own bedroom door across the hall. But at the sound of his father's calling, John leapt from Lise's bed and tried to pull on his pants, which tangled. Then Lise's door opened, and there was his father's face. His real face.

"Lise, where's . . . oh." Mr. Collin closed the door, stood behind it silently a moment, then announced, "John, I want to talk to you, downstairs."

The lecture took place at the breakfast table, over eggs and oatmeal mush. Father and son, alone. At John's entrance, Mr. Collin dismissed his wife with a monotone explanation that, dear, he had to speak with his son, that there were some things a mother could not. . . . But Alicia was already up and out, the door clicking softly behind her.

Not knowing if he was supposed to eat the food in

front of him, John listened to his father unfurl his argument. He sounded very serious. His eyes were clear, and only his mouth moved as he spoke. He wiped his egg spoon clean, and then tapped the table with it, sharply, to make final certain points. He explained to his son about hired help. He explained about racial barriers, about "embarrassing complications." He told John that Lise would have to be "let go". He paused to watch John, whose face showed him nothing at all. Then his monotone changed, somewhat, and he reddened, a sad grin wavering at the corners of his mouth.

"Do you . . . sleep in her bed . . . often?" he asked, and then bowed his head, chuckled, and began to eat his eggs again.

"No," answered John, truthfully enough. For usually they did their "love dancing" (as they called it) in his bed after school, or outside during good weather. They'd never slept together before.

His father seemed satisfied. His next question, though, puzzled John.

"So, she likes hockey players, does she?" He laughed and shook his head, then began spooning his mush in huge gulps.

"Well," John said, "she likes me, I guess." Something told him it was best not to mention how she'd been talking to him lately, strangely, always about love. Instead, copying his father's example, he chuckled too and began to eat.

"Before I met your mother, son . . . in Winnipeg . . . there were girls . . . girls, by god, who you wouldn't . . . ," but he stopped there. John had stopped eating. His spoon, full of egg, he held motionless a few inches from his mouth. His eyes—uncomprehending, but eager—were fixed on his father's face.

The day after his father's discovery, John found a note from Lise tucked in his lunch bag, asking if he felt like "tunnel-dancing" that afternoon before hockey practice.

"Yes," thought John. He could not imagine any other answer. Meeting Lise meant skipping dinner, but then his stomach never wanted much to do with hockey after a dinner anyway. Lise, and hockey: his body wanted both equally.

They met outside the library. An early darkness, and off in the northern pitch a budding line of green-gold borealis hung hissing. A wind had gathered as well, which froze their cheeks and stung them with unseen ice crystals.

"A tunnel is so much nicer when it's so windy," said Lise, when they were poking about for an old tunnel by the hockey rink, "especially when you hear it blowing. It feels so cosy then. In the snow." John thought he could see what she meant, so he agreed.

"So what did your dad say to you?" Lise asked.

"When?"

"Yesterday, dumb boy, after he saw us in my bed."

"I was out of the bed."

"Well he knew you were just *in* the bed. *Jesus!* So what did he say?" Lise's stick had found the drifted-over entrance to their tunnel. As she hunched like a digging dog, the snow shot rhythmically and at an angry speed from between her legs. John had to step aside.

"He said I had to be careful because you are Métis, because you are our servant girl, and. . . ."

"But was he mad!"

"No, I don't think so. He said you were 'let go', but his face said he was lying again. He said a lot of things. I didn't get much. He asked if you liked hockey players."

"So you aren't going to be punished?"

"I don't think so. Why?" Lise kept carving out the

edges of the hole she'd uncovered. Her shoulders sagged slightly as she sighed her "English girl's sigh", as John called it.

"But isn't that good he wasn't mad?" John asked, puzzled now.

"Did you bring the candle? Give it to me, and the matches."

"Here. But isn't it good?"

"Christ almighty! *Jesus!*" hissed Lise, who then crossed herself and mumbled something. "Just come in, okay? We'll talk about it."

The last thing John wanted was more "talk about it". It had been hard enough yesterday, listening to his father. And now Lise: week after week she was getting harder to understand.

She had changed so much in the past year, since their first "dance", and John could not begin to see the reasons. She was still Lise but . . . something was missing, and something new was getting bigger. It was at least a year since she'd sneaked into the bathroom where, giggling, she'd bent him over to wipe him clean, saying, "Just like I used to, you dirty dumb boy, do you remember?" It was a year ago that she'd given up telling stories about the messy love disasters of her old schoolgirl friends. And, lately, she no longer teased him about his own goat-clumsy performance as they "danced" in those shadowy secret spots. These days she seemed disappointed, her sighs off-key as she demanded more from him, saying testily, "No, men do it *this* way."

Something had been added. A lie. John knew the lie came from the books she read, and the new movies the Rialto was showing. And the magic that lit her eyes when she told him about the books, about the movies, about her future—that same magical light he once thought was her delight and her wisdom—he now saw to be the light of a lie. He saw it often: a dream, a lie, focused in the air around her face. It jumped and sparkled there as though her lie had grown a faint, giddy halo.

Why did she lie? Did she know she lied? John knew he was far from understanding her. But, he thought now, following on all fours her bear-like bum into the tunnel, he was nowhere near understanding lots of things. All he knew—and here he pictured her bum being led by a face that radiated a magical, lying light which pierced the darkness of the snow bedroom—all he knew was that he didn't like being lied to.

He would rather just dance with her, here in the tunnel. He would rather just dance than have to pretend he was a lord who had asked her, a countess, to tea. He would rather just call her Lise than Maude or Becky. Or Tess. He especially hated when she played Tess, for that meant he had to be Angel Claire, who Lise seemed to know everything about—how he kissed, what he said, how his religious eyes shone a weird light on sex—and so she always found fault with John's performance.

No, John would simply rather tunnel-dance, rather just enjoy the difference of a woman's body, a difference—if she stood a certain way, with breasts and curves just so—that made a woman's body reach out and nudge everything in a room, whereas a man's body just sat inside whatever he was wearing.

But now, in their snow bedroom, Lise wanted more talk. John was already tickling her under her pants, but she seemed bored. She told him she was glad he hadn't been punished, but it was "well . . . too bad" that Mr. Collin wasn't angry with them.

"Why?" asked John, for what she'd just said went against all he'd been told about duty to parents. He withdrew his hand, puzzled, but Lise caught it and put it back in place.

"Well, it would have made it . . . *this* . . . better."

"Oh."

"But your father thinks it's okay."

"I don't know what he thinks."

"Well, it makes me feel like a *whore!*" Lise crossed herself and whispered something again. John still didn't know what to say, but thought it might be a good time for a joke. He wasn't at all sure with jokes, so he made himself chuckle first—to tell her a joke was coming—and then he tried it:

"A whore who likes hockey players!" he laughed.

Lise pushed his hand away and screamed at him. Then she started crying, and cried for a long while. Her sobs, John saw, made the snow room so different from before. It was usually such a quick place, where a candle flickered, where they tickled each other, and danced, and Lise groaned and laughed, and both their bodies shook. Now, as though Lise's whimpers were only a small thing coming from a distant corner, the room was made quiet and vast. The candle throbbed weakly.

Confusing. Lise was lying again, this time to herself only, and this time more than ever. Huddled in the snow, she rocked and groaned. In pain. An act, and yet not at all an act. In pain.

John recalled their only meeting with Bert Flute this past spring. The old hobo had been nervous; he laughed and jerked constantly and punched the air many times, yelling, "The air's fulla fock!" He'd begun touching Lise, laughing, and then groping at her, crying. When, queenly, Lise rebuffed him, he got mad and started to shake, and turned his back on them. When he pivoted to face them again he had his penis out, resting limply on his chicken hand.

"Here!" he cried, "Here! Look at Flute, see what be hangin' off his soul!"

John looked at the penis, smooth and pink, blind and stupid, like something that grew quietly out of a lake bed, like a clam-tongue. Standing there, watching it, John knew its two-fold purpose—and Bert Flute's penis seemed to know too, for it began to grow hard.

In the flickering snow room, John waited calmly beside Lise. When he heard the first faint shouts, and the sharp, echoing clatter of pucks and sticks on the distant rink boards, he knew that his hockey practice had begun, and that their tunnel-dance had failed and was over. He tapped Lise on the shoulder, but she only grunted angrily and shrugged his hand away.

John settled back and listened to the rink noises, which sounded like precise clicks mixed with dull, ghostly booms. He heard a whistle blow: the noise stopped. John looked down at Lise and moved to touch her again, but withdrew, unsure. Then a clear thought came: if only this *love* was like hockey. Hockey, with its rules, its goals, off-sides. Teams that shook hands.

Love might be like that too, he decided, if you took the lies out of it. For it too was fast and clean like hockey, and brought on the same kind of stomach juice of motion and pleasure. But both things, love and hockey, were ruined by people who couldn't keep things straight. Because hockey was ruined too. Not the game, the game was okay: the people weren't.

The distant whistle shrieked again, and John's body jumped in response. Listening to the shouts and clicks again, he managed a picture of himself playing. So fast and right, the skating, the shooting, the passing. His body could taste it. Only when a goal was scored and the play stopped, only when he went to the bench for a rest did the trouble start. There he didn't fit in at all, for there the game was changed completely.

On the bench: the others beside him always managed to stay *in* the game. They shouted, cheered, swore, jerked about like the bench was hot, followed the puck and flashing bodies with eyes that seemed attached to the play by some relentless nerve. But for John the bench meant only . . . well, the bench. He could jerk about like the others, but what for?

When he first started playing he'd been told that the bench was for "catching your breath". Easy enough to understand: on the ice he got tired. But to this day, years later, "catching his breath" was all John could get himself to do on the bench.

Not only could he see no reason in jumping and shouting, but the seemingly simple act of catching up to his lost breath occupied him entirely. For it was a most spectacular thing: here was his body, a body with a one-track mind, convulsing and sucking at that whole expanse of air. So hungry for air the animal is panicking. Its fighting for breath reminded John of a pig at its trough, so greedy in its spasm for food that its legs quiver.

So John would be on the bench, not noticing the game going on just over the boards; he'd gulp air, and think how air was like food, and think how his pig-body's snout was forever plugged into the endless trough out there. And how inside of him he carried an empty bag that was always filling up and emptying, filling up, emptying, on and on, even while he slept: for a lifetime he would be plugged into this invisible pig's-food. He could only stop when he swallowed, or pinched his nostrils. He was a pig that never got enough to eat. And he would think how, if he was really supposed to join in and talk to his team-mates, instead of complaining, between breaths, how dirty number six was, or how Donny Beamer was a puck-hog, he'd much rather talk with them about how exciting it was, wasn't it, to watch their own, small, panicking bags of air having such a hard, quivering time of it catching up to the grand steadiness of air above the lights of the hockey rink. He often wanted to poke someone in the ribs (like the other boys did to each other) and tell him about it. But he already knew what the reaction would be. And, besides, something would always happen, someone would score and, knowing what was expected of him, John would have to cheer, and pound on somebody's back. An easy act. Easy to lie, to show breathless joy, when breathless is what you already really are.

The candle danced fitfully, on the verge of going out. John couldn't help but watch his shadow as it jumped on the snow wall beside him, turning from black to grey to black again in rhythm to the leaping flame. The sight almost made him sick: for one moment his stomach couldn't understand how this room, so perfectly silent and still, could at the same time be so jerky. But Lise had stopped crying at last. One of her English-girl sighs told him that things had settled again, that the lie, anyway, was back to normal. John moved closer to her, grunting softly as he did, and slid his hand back into her pants.

"*Jesus* . . . !" Lise cried. She slapped his hand away hard, and then scooped up a wedge of snow and flung it in his face. She jumped to her knees, and with contorted, whirlwind arms clawed a blizzard of snow chunks at him. At first John protected himself, not knowing what to do. Then, wondering if this might not be a game after all, grunting and giggling he flailed away himself and pelted Lise in return.

In the middle of the flurry Lise stopped, and John's last wad of snow burst apart on her face. With crumbling snow caught in her hair, and a ridge of snow that rode inside her lower lip, that hesitated and then began to melt quickly, Lise stared at John. John's smile dropped. They stared at one another for several moments, breathing hard. John watched as a quiver in Lise's chin worked up to her mouth, made it jerk and then open into a contorted, hideous kind of smile which, still moving up, made her cheeks tighten, forced her eyes to shut and then tears to start. She began to sob again, quietly, and as she cried she brought both hands to her lap and began doing up her zipper. She struggled with it, wriggling her hips this way and that, but her fingers were numb and stupid and there was snow in the zipper teeth. Her fight to close it became more and more frantic until finally she screamed, and jumped to her feet, and in doing so she punched her head through the snow ceiling.

It was an odd sight for John. As soon as Lise's head disappeared up through the snow, she stopped moving— except for her hands, which fell away from her zipper to her sides. There she stood, as if she was calm, as if she had no head, as if her head was completely obscured by a layer of cloud. Not wanting to provoke her again, John did nothing, but after a silent minute had passed between him and this headless girl he felt forced to speak. And her pants were falling down her thighs.

"Lise?"

"Shut up. Get out." Coming from outside the room Lise's voice was muted, ghostly.

"What are you doing? Isn't it time to go?"

"You go."

John sat still for another minute. Then he tried again. "Lise?"

"Get out. Now. I never want to talk to you again."

John paused, then did up his coat and started crawling out the tunnel-way. He wondered what he was going to do: his hockey practice was probably more than half over. Emerging from the tunnel he stood, turned, and was almost surprised by the disembodied head sitting upright on the snow eight feet away. Lise was staring up at the wide, black dome of prairie sky. He heard her whisper to herself, in that English-girl accent, "It seems I have such great white shoulders. . . ." Her mouth hung a little slack, and her eyes moved from east to west in a slow, slow arc. Her head was framed by a ten-foot circle of faint, yellow light, which flickered.

"Lise, should I put out the candle?"

"I don't care. Go away."

John chose to walk home over the farmers' fields. The night was growing colder, and his boots crunched through the ice crust that had formed on the snow. He felt how the air burned as he pulled it through his nostrils, how it burned a little less in his throat and how it felt neither warm nor cold as it filled his chest. He watched the snow fields around him bounce as he walked, watched the smooth plane of snow approach him, watched and felt his boots crush through it. Strange, though, with all he saw and felt, how often a vision of Lise's head burst through and confused what was really there.

WHY THE RETARDED ARE HERE ON EARTH

It was this year's Christmas party. With dusty streamers taped in an asymmetrical weave overhead, and rough paper snowflakes hanging everywhere, and the weight of so many ugly, home-made ornaments bending tree branches almost to the floor, it looked just like last year.

That was one of the points of the exercise: even though it doomed a party to ugliness, you let them do decorations and hors d'oeuvres and such themselves. Russ would sometimes argue this point with Patricia.

When Russ walked in and saw the room and heard the familiar artless voices rise in a wall of greeting, he felt instantly tired. More tired—he saw with a surge of guilt—because unlike last year's party he wasn't being paid. This was a Saturday night freebie at the group home.

Roy Orbison wailed his celebrated sadness. It was the only music Russ had heard here in weeks. There stood Arthur, guarding the stereo. Arthur owned the album collection, a large one handed down to him by a brother moved to Europe. And Russ had found it fun for a while, rediscovering the likes of Gene Pitney and The Kinks and even The Fuggs. But when told of Orbison's death Arthur took to playing nothing else. He'd recently sat through a TV tribute to John Lennon, so there might have been some confusion. Or maybe he thought that death meant you were supposed to think of them more than ever. Arthur had a fully functional stubborn streak, coupled with a dark mis-trust of most everything. He dwelled in a state that could be trained but not reasoned with. But tonight Russ found the music appropriate for once. This party was definitely more Orbison than Jingle Bells.

He saw Peter and Julie at the punch bowl. They were chipper, it was their shift, they were making money and their smiles were made somewhat easy by this. The only difference between them and Russ was that Russ and the other off-duty staff could get a bit drunker. But they were all at work. Talking to anyone here, even the parents, meant work.

Sally, mongoloid, a big moon-sweet face, proudly held a tray of pink punch up to him. The tray tilted dangerously. She grunted but got the inflection right, an offering. Russ took a glass and secreted his other hand under the tray to keep it level while she lowered it. She didn't notice. He thanked her and wished her Merry Christmas. Sally echoed his wish with a four-syllable grunt, matching his tone perfectly. Off to the side another off-duty staffer, Bill, waved him over.

Russ followed Bill into the work room where the bottle was. He swallowed half his punch and topped up with vodka. How long, Bill was wondering, do you think we should stick this one out? Until Patricia leaves I guess, Russ said, though they both knew this. As supervisor, Patricia was tyrannical toward staff. But since the tyranny sprang from nothing but an inexhaustible kindness toward these folks, mutiny was not possible. Even hard gossip about Patricia made Russ uneasy. She was so good at her job.

Maybe, Bill said, tilting the vodka bottle for a swig, and waggling his eyebrows in Groucho Marx lechery, she'll bring a date tonight and leave early for her Christmas present.

Everyone had to be as giving. If not, her punishment was the surprise on her face, then a slow turning away, a display of an awesome sadness, her damned doe-eyes filled with the discovery that these trusting, forgotten people weren't getting the love they needed to survive. That look had more than once made Russ feel like a sweating, pinching, greedy man.

Back in the party room, moon-faced Sally was dancing with her father. Russ didn't care to watch her moves. Her grotesque interpretation of what was cool made him queasy. There, a few pelvis thrusts, which her father laughed at, though he looked queasy too, and god only knew if she understood what they were about.

Suddenly Wing was on his arm, shouting, "*Merry Xmas, Rusty*"! Playfully stressing the X. He was twenty, Chinese. His first name was Danny but he was always just Wing, the perfect name for him. He had a very normal, in fact a delightful, sense of humour. He'd get obsessed with things. Rock stars. Social work. Lately he'd been going to church and a special Sunday school, and returned spouting religious sayings, always mangling, always distorting. He'd eat, for instance, and look at his stomach and say, "God is in us."

Wing was his favourite, though his tone of voice was an eerie kind of baby talk.

"Rusty," Wing shouted at him again for the tenth time that week, "Tuesday's the big birthday!"

That's right, Wing, Christmas, Russ said. He waited for the next bit.

"And X marks the spot!" Wing drove a finger into his palm, and laughed.

Russ wasn't sure what this was about. It was either a play on the Xmas, or about the three kings following the star, finding the manger.

It was hard to categorize his problem. Typical of Wing was to open a can of beans and pour it into a paper bag the morning of a picnic, and this after a week of sandwich-making lessons. Russ often found him up at three a.m. having breakfast. He would ride a bus for hours at a time, stimming out on shape and colour mutating through the foggy square of glass, until the driver figured him out and phoned. Bus drivers got a lot of that.

But Russ thought that Wing and he could almost be, well, friends. The others he pitied, and loved. Sure, he could use the word love. Love, and hate. The happy-face social worker smile goes away quickly. Familiarity breeds. He was finally honest about this.

But with Wing, sometimes Russ could look into Wing's eyes and know that he knew.

Wing didn't belong here with these others. But where else would he go?

"Getting drunk again Rusty?" Wing teased.

A good memory too. Last year, this same party, this same room, though on duty Russ had gotten a little loose. Patricia had looked on the verge of giving him the dread sad-eyes, until she saw how much they all loved this looser Russ. Or, perhaps, how much more a looser Russ loved them.

"Let's have a wing-ding!" Wing was yelling now.

Let's get wingy and have a wing-ding, Wing-man, Russ said.

"It's party time!" Wing yelled. "Gimme five!" he yelled next, holding out his hand. Russ gave him five. Wing would stretch this thing as far as Russ let him.

"Gimme ten!" He held out two hands. Next he'd be on his back with his feet in the air, asking for fifteen, then twenty. It was a funny enough joke, but not for the hundredth time. Russ gave him his ten, then said, Gotta go,

Wing-man. He turned away as if he had something official to do. Give them an inch, he found himself thinking, even Wing. Then he felt guilty thinking it.

Walking past the stereo Russ noticed Roy Orbison was wailing louder, the volume rule knowingly breached. Jesus, give them an inch. He edged the volume knob down. He shook his head at Arthur.

There was Patricia at the door saying sorry she was late. Julie, on duty, took her and her date's coat (she had a date!) and then Patricia started in on kissing everyone, parents and staff too. Her date, a quite fat man introduced to the group as Dean, kept up a smile though he was clearly afraid. Russ wondered if Patricia had given big Dean a pep talk, if she'd told him her favourite thing to tell: There are no rules in this house except intelligence and kindness. The other thing she liked to say was: You can see yourself in them.

In the five years he'd been here Russ had brought over a few friends too. They'd looked identically afraid. Scared they'd make some kind of faux pas. Which was funny, because these were the weakest people in the world, their lives a never-ending string of faux pas.

Patricia gave Russ his smooch. Her bright eyes and genuine smile followed, and Russ did his best to return it all.

Have you sung carols yet? she asked him. He told her no, and she said good. He asked if he should put on that Christmas record, that old Mitch Miller, to sing along to. He turned and went for it. No, it'll drown them out, she said to his back.

Russ changed course mid-step, and headed to the work room for a refill, shaking his head. Christ, he had to get out of here. He admitted to himself that that had been his desire, of course, to hear Mitch Miller rather than them. Mitch Miller was bad enough. He looked back for Bill. He refused to feel guilty any more this evening. He resigned himself to an hour of straining noise, of kaleidoscopic tunelessness.

Bill was already in the work room knifing the plastic off a new bottle top, rum now. I promised Wing a bit, Bill said, and poured some into a glass of punch.

Russ was going to tell him about the weird new medication Wing was on these days, but of course Bill knew that. Instead he said, "They don't metabolize."

"What?"

"Orientals. They don't metabolize alcohol as well as we do. Don't give him much."

Bill lifted the punch glass impatiently. "I didn't."

"Well don't." Jesus, why had he said that?

Bill brushed past him with two glasses of Christmas cheer.

"You shouldn't quit, man," Bill said. "You've been talking about it for a hundred years."

"You know, she brought a date," Russ said quickly, trying to fix things. Not turning to look at him, Bill said he knew that, and then Bill disappeared out into a huge silent room which at that instant broke into the ugliest, slowest version of Deck the Halls ever sung.

Maybe he'd been jealous that Wing, his favourite, his friend, had asked Bill for the drink and not him. Maybe he'd just been working here too long. Burn-out. Why did he work here? What was the point of it? These people knew their lives were bad. Everything they attempted and couldn't do reminded them of this. No one was getting better, no matter how many tuna casserole lessons they got, no matter how much love.

Russ decided to go for a walk. He could not stand the noise, this noise in particular. Patricia wouldn't miss him. Singing was her favourite thing on nights like this, which was funny as hell because she couldn't carry a tune either. But she'd be in there warbling her head off, catching people's eyes and smiling, setting an example of proper Christmas joy.

He took a deep pull of rum, shuddered and went out the back door. The singing faded. If anything, such noise was good in that it showed—in this case screamed—what good music could be. A bad thing always hinted its opposite. Like this job made you think of a better one. Like Young Cooks Tuna Bake made you appreciate something delicious.

Another thing Patricia liked to say was: They will make you feel lucky.

He stayed away exactly an hour and a half. On his walk back from the bar it was snowing heavily, and twice he barely caught himself mid-slip. It was the dress shoes, he wasn't drunk.

One time Russ nearly slipped while laughing out loud at what Wing had said this morning at breakfast, as his shift ended. All week Wing had been mimicking someone, probably his Sunday school teacher, and he'd ask Russ in a formal tone, Do you know why the retarded are here on Earth? (Only a Sunday school teacher could say such an incorrect thing and get away with it.) And this morning Wing had come up with a new one. It was hard to say whether or not he was trying to be funny, but as he stood in the kitchen, pointing at the horrendous breakfast mess and the bodies slouched around the table slurping up cereal, he announced, "I'd be worried if I was God." And then, even better, Arthur picked up his head and said, in a bored, superior voice, "You're Chinese."

He arrived, brushed snowflakes off his coat. Evidence. From the work room it sounded like a real party going on. He went in. Barry Manilow's Christmas was on but could hardly be heard over the screeching and laughter. Arthur bobbed catatonic beside the stereo. People danced in twos and threes and alone. Judging from the rhythms they moved to, they heard a private music. A few still sung carols. The fat date, Dean, had a ring of people around him, a mix of parents and staff mostly, all smiling. He was telling jokes. He must be good—some were laughing even before the next punch line came. Patricia, holding his hand, was wiping a tear and groaning from the last one.

Wing came roaring out of nowhere and had Russ by the arm. He tried to spin him as in a square dance.

"Do the shingaling witha Wingaling!" he yelled, pulling.

He looked drunk. He looked very happy, but in a desperate, hyperactive way. His teeth were clenched.

"I threw up!" he yelled, sounding proud.

"Does Bill know?"

"Bill told me it's all under control!"

Russ danced himself away from Wing and looked for Bill. He avoided Patricia's eyes. He found Julie and asked her if she'd seen him and was told Bill had left a while ago. Then Russ asked her if she'd by any chance given Wing any booze. One or two little drinks, yes, she said, why? But Russ was already calculating in his head, seven staff times one or two little drinks apiece equals what?

Now parents were putting on coats. Noise down, party over. Someone plucked the needle off Barry Manilow. It was almost as though a whistle had blown. The residents accepted this. In their world, parties were turned off. Lights went up. A balloon popped, then another. People stood at the door, sighing and laughing still, saying great party and thanking Patricia and hugging the child or brother or sister who lived here.

Russ stood in the middle of the room, looking down, tapping a foot. He wondered what he'd do when he got home. He wished he hadn't had quite so much to drink. When he looked up, there was Patricia smiling at him from across the room, sighing visibly for him, then a thumbs-up sign. We did okay, she was saying. God, those eyes. She was looking at him just like she looked at them.

"Let's get him!" Wing shouted. Russ turned and six or seven of them were on him, grabbing his arms and wrapping him up with dusty streamers. Tie him up tight, he heard Patricia yelling from across the room.

Laughing exactly like children, they wrapped his ankles, his arms. He let himself be pushed to the floor. Now a streamer went around his mouth, muffling his nervous, high-pitched giggle. He could taste cake icing on it. Wing hissed the conspiracy in his ear, "Patricia said it's our job to bug you, Rusty!"

Laughter, shrieks, grunts. Someone echoed, "It's our job!" Russ was now bound by enough crêpe that he could not resist if he wanted to. A streamer went round his neck, tight enough to scare him. He grunted a warning plea. All he could do was grunt, and moan. A streamer went over his eyes, blocking out the world: a sweet moon-face, a bent forehead, squinting eyes and weird mouths wet and open in their fun.

BIG ANIMALS

This is a stupid story, because it's about stupid people. Though it has a stupid ending as well—someone named Chip loses his left buttock to a bear—it's not a simple story. It shows how complicated stupidity can get.

First, my wife Rose was stupid to have her little affair. And I was stupid to run away like that, like a kicked dog looking back over its shoulder, showing teeth.

Because her fling made sense, at least to her. She said, "It was needed," and "We'll be better for it." I should have listened, Rose doesn't lie. But her words had less chance cooling my heart than a feather does a volcano. Jealousy may be stupid, but it has the brute strength to squeeze the world.

* * *

I fled Vancouver for a logging camp in the Squamish Valley. Such work dulls a past, and at the same time gives crumbs of worth. You can act morose, eccentric, rabid, but if you do your work, people let you be. Here's the kind of place it was: the owner of Squamish Timber himself once had a few beers and ordered a small mountain be given a Mohawk. The crew was a month into the shave before a tree planter found out and called Victoria.

Logging was as different as possible from the work

I'd left behind in the Physics Department, which was maybe why I chose it. I was a chokerman, the worst job of all. There's the frantic rush to pull a steel cable "as thick as a good dick" into and over and under a jumble of crazy-fallen, teetering logs, looking for one to "choke" so it can be dragged uphill. The whole show waits for the chokermen to do this. Expensive machines are in neutral.

Then comes a minute of absolute idleness while the logs are hauled up and unhitched and loaded. Choking is a jarring job—either everything is happening or nothing at all. The point is, chokermen are forced by sudden silence to catch their breath and think on things.

The nature of chokermen's thoughts? The usual, the football scores, or how each few minutes means another buck in the wallet. Or hating a foreman. Or danger (a chokerman was just killed in the next valley down), or lunch waiting in a bag in the crew truck. Some, perhaps fugitives like me, wore ironic looks on their faces, and had thoughts that appeared to curl off on angles that would never be talked about. Me, I thought about Rose.

* * *

The pay phone was just inside the machine shop. You could stand outside around the corner and eavesdrop unseen from three feet away. This had the effect of making everyone careful about what they said, and often whisper. I was surprised no one complained. It was as if, by complaining, a man admitted he had secrets from the other men. Or worse, that he spoke to his wife in a fancy or whiny way he didn't want the men to hear. It was this silliest of fears that killed my first call.

I had one more number to push when it struck me that I had no clue how this might go. (And I could hear a boot outside, dragging a rhythm in the dust.) Would we yell? Would I whine? Or, god, cry?

In the curt talk we'd ended on in our kitchen, she'd shown compassion for me, but no apology. It felt like a contradiction: just screwed by another, yet gazing on me with loving concern.

I still hadn't punched the last number when a guy I didn't know poked his head in. My hand may have been shaking on the receiver. I hung up with a "damn, can't remember the number" look, and that was that.

* * *

The Squamish Valley can probably be seen from space. It is rimmed by five small glaciers, some of which glow turquoise at their centres, depending on the time of day. Eagles hang in a sky so blue it threatens violet. One thing we loggers had in common was that it was hard to shake off the roar and tangle and thoughts, to look up and realize yet again: how beautiful.

The gist of our work was a slaughterhouse, a vegetable abattoir, and the turpentine smell of sap—tree blood— was sharp in the air, testimony to the shocked death of acre after acre of noble, healthy, centuries-old trees. The smell burns nostrils, and even after it's gotten used to, it keeps men dizzy. It was hard to look up from this smell, or from the miles of bleeding trees, clanking machinery and men who pissed where they stood.

So we were a mess trapped in this beautiful bowl. I sometimes see this bowl as a microcosm for a trapped humanity, but then I'm not so sure. I think, again, the people in this story are simply stupider than usual.

* * *

Since we were three hours from Vancouver and most men drove home on weekends, the camp didn't qualify as Isolation, with the perks that come with that. Oddly, the farther into the bush you went, the cushier it got. Camps in the middlest of nowhere had French chefs, good movies, and hookers flown in. There, camp life meant drinking and playing cards for money. Stories about such camps were rife with greed and agony and stupidity. Most were here at this "dry" camp because they wanted it, having tried the other life and lost.

But there was nothing to do. For a volleyball court someone had stolen an Indian's net from downriver and strung it across beheaded saplings. I never saw anyone use it. There was a rec-shack with old pool table, pocked dart board and koolaid cooler. Dusty baseball mitts lay in a corner beside a bat carved with a chainsaw. The ball had been slugged into the river by a recently fired, mythical behemoth named Clarkie. Now the only ballgame was to joke about how far the ball had made it downstream and out to sea: Clarkie's infinite home run.

Once a week in the rec-shack they ran a movie on a projector. Wary of getting a campful of men riled over women, the company sent only old cowboy and gangster shows, the kind where car tires squeal on gravel, music wows, and scotch-tape splices "pop" out whole bits of dialogue. At some point the cook—angry because this was beneath him—stomped in with popcorn. After the movie someone would bring up the rumour of the new VCR and TV and dish. This rumour was years old. But whenever the lights came on and everyone saw the dime-size holes where darts had gone through the screen, and felt in their bones the mediocrity of what they'd just watched, and the aloofness of a company that didn't care to give them anything more than this, it was automatic that they had to talk about something better.

Some men tried hikes through the beauty, but to loggers that was a busman's holiday. Why stomp bush for free? One mechanic spent his off time tying trout flies. One guy was finishing grade twelve by mail, and another had trained himself to sleep almost all the time. Once I saw two men in the woods stroking each other. A few men I think stayed secretly drunk. Two chokermen, Chuck and Dale, or Chip and Dale as we knew them, ran a pot farm on the fireweed slopes.

* * *

I may have gone a bit insane at one point. I hallucinated sex. I don't know why. Jealousy? Altitude? Or could the cause have been as stupid as not having had sex for a month? In any case, like all hallucinations (I've read), it felt like truth.

We were up the west slope near the snow line, and the loader horn blew lunch. I'd been thinking of her, thinking in particular of her and him, seeing them both naked, moving, making noises. I knew her noises so well. And her smell. A pure rage gripped me. It was as if I was addicted to these images.

I recall this: suffering another vision of them mating, I closed my eyes and took a deep breath. There was hope in the breath, me trying to draw something in. But when I opened my eyes, the billowed clouds above me were shifting in sexual contortions. I couldn't make out everything—the clouds hid the worst of it behind the puffy façade—but I knew what was going on. Worse, they were juvenile and playful: dirty bouncing puppy games.

I vaguely came to realize I was standing there, jealous of clouds. Feeling foolish, I shook my head to clear it. It didn't help. Now the trees edging the cut were abuzz with sex: their one urge was to strain to be greener and taller and more in the sun so as to flourish and sprawl and spew pollen.

I was breathing hard, and I was worried. Closing my eyes made it worse, for my feet could feel the undulations of the valley itself. I could sense entire mountain slopes joining deep underground beneath the valley floor, excited at where they met at a fissure. My stomach became the jealous fulcrum for grinding rock slabs, miles in size. The sex of mountains. The infidelity of the earth's crust.

* * *

On my third weekend there Chip and Dale introduced themselves. I'd been avoiding it, but it was inevitable. Of the forty men, only three of us—Chip, Dale and I—had nothing better to do than stay there on weekends.

For me it was a case of no other place to go. This notion helped fire my self-pity as I walked endless miles of path and riverbank surrounding the camp. The glaciers and towering cedar made my anguish feel airy and noble for a time, but soon I was bored with it. On the third Saturday morning I walked only as far as the rec-shack, drawn by dumb instinct to the clack of billiard balls, and curses.

Chip was short and stupid, and Dale was tall and stupider. They looked about twenty-five. Both utterly lacked charisma. They shared a nasty humour and were always elbowing and insulting each other: they were the kind of best friends who called each other asshole, but not smiling. They also shared a love of breaking things. Non-stop, unconscious, in passing: darts chocked into walls, styrofoam cups crushed in hands, leaves torn from any bush passed by. All while carrying on a stupid banter. In minutes I saw exactly what they were. They were mean nerds.

That first day I shot a game of pool with them, not saying much. They had a whispered argument—every word of which I could hear—about whether or not to let me see "the plantation". I heard things like: "There's no way he's a cop, you asshole." "He might rip some off." "He's straight, probably never even smokes." "We blindfold him, right? Hah hah!"

They broke their huddle and asked me if I'd help carry some water to their garden. On the mile-long hike, each of us lugging two plastic jugs, I noticed some of their differences. Chip had a babyish body, bad teeth and was constantly sarcastic. Tall Dale wore glasses and a soulless, icy look whenever he wasn't giggling at some remark of Chip's. He tried to copy his short friend's wit but couldn't, so he giggled. For a tall man he had a disproportionately small head.

They asked questions that had apparently been stewing.

"So, you don't seem like a bush type guy, eh?" Chip said.

"Dunno," I answered. For three weeks I'd been trying not to act or talk like a doctoral candidate in physics. To draw less attention I'd been honing the rhythms of rough talk.

"Well why you here then?" asked Dale, impatient.

"You don't ask like that, asshole," Chip told him, only half smiling. "He might be hiding from some, some traffic violation, right?" He elbowed me and laughed at his subtle joke.

Dale giggled.

"My wife and I...." Why was I saying this? To them! Well, why not? This was as harmless as venting to a couple of stumps. "We had a fight. Plus I need some money to finish school."

"Gettin your trade, eh? What school?" asked Chip. Before I could think how to answer, and to my relief, he continued. "Went for a machinist's ticket myself couple years back. All paid for. But I quit the fucker."

"Probbly got kicked out," said Dale, slouching beside us.

"Yeah right, asshole," said Chip.

"Probbly couldn't even spell," said Dale.

"Yeah right. Listen to a guy who can't even spell Fuck Me."

"Fuck *you*," said Dale. Then he giggled because he thought he'd got a good one in.

I felt lucky to escape having to explain my trade: non-gravitational accelerated electromagnetism.

* * *

Rose was at UBC too. Her lover, Barto Kovic, was a physics professor, a man from whom I'd taken courses, a man with whom I'd sipped wine in the kitchens of department parties.

Everyone knew what was going on. In a quickly called meeting with my advisers, me requesting time off, they'd nodded and asked too few questions. I sensed conspiracy. I could picture smiling Barto Kovic telling them, "Make it easy for him to leave."

Thoughts of going back to Rose led to thoughts of going back to all of them. They'd always know. They'd know she gleefully screwed another man. They'd know I bowed my head and came back.

Why did this matter to me? What was it about appearances? We were physicists. Quick glances, genitalia, pure emotion—nothing this savage had anything to do with physics.

* * *

Chip said, "Hope it's okay it's marijuana we're gonna water," in tones that hid neither the boast nor the intent to shock. They looked disappointed that I already knew. It was funny that what did end up shocking me, they treated so casually.

We'd reached the farm, announced Dale, and I got my shock. A sudden smell of rotten meat, and then I saw the bear head impaled on a pole. From the mouth hung a bluish tongue, dried to leather. The eyes were gone, and a wasp flew out of an ear.

Chuck saw me staring. In an "oh, that," tone, he chanted, "A-bear-a-year-keeps-our-pot-plants-here." Dale's giggle sounded tired. He'd no doubt heard that one a lot.

"Actually," Chip said, "we only need a head when plants're small, keep deers an' shit away. So we won't shoot another one till next springtime." To ease my disappointment over this, he added, "Wanna come? I got a twelve-gauge. Knock 'em out of a tree, right up close."

His manner took for granted that anyone who ended up here, choking logs and staying weekends, would love to shoot a treed bear, hack its head off and ram it on a pole. I grunted vaguely.

They had a "quarter thousand" plants hidden in the fireweed. They only had to worry in the fall when the marijuana went darker and grew taller than fireweed and could maybe be spotted from the air. Dale whispered that they used planes in California, and did I know that the FBI ran the RCMP? But they wouldn't get caught, said Chip. A cousin was coming in two months to pick it and take it to town.

"He even planted it," Dale said. "Alls we do is grow it."

We watered the ten or so plants that had been planted on a ridge of earth and so didn't get enough ground water. I wondered if they or the cousin had figured out why these plants were smaller than the others.

"Big money here in this field," said Dale, his voice falling to a sagely tone I was to hear whenever he passed on any grandfatherly cliché. He added another one, in the same tone. "It's a dangerous . . . business."

"Both of us got cars with it last year," Chip announced. "His," he put an elbow in Dale's ribs, "is a piece of shit."

"Eat me," said Dale, not smiling.

* * *

My walks narrowed to two favourite spots. One was a bend in the river where the water deepened and darkened. The bank was overhung with pine boughs. In this charmed enclosure I sat on the sand and watched trout rise.

Here, I tried not to think about Rose. Though I was a scientist who knew better, I viewed my predicament in archaic terms: here was earth under me, here was air around me, here was water flowing by and here was fire inside. It was so quiet by this river. Basic things were easy to see.

I'd spoken with her. My worst rage had been snuffed by her damned reasonableness. "It was juvenile," she said. "It meant nothing. I came out not liking him at all. You have to believe me when I say it's helped how I feel about you." In her voice, all logic. Still no apology.

"How many times," I found myself asking, "did you do it with him?" She fell silent at this, maybe realizing for the first time what she was dealing with here, what part of me.

My other walk was to the camp dump, to see the bears. There was nothing quiet about that festering place, nor did it aid thinking. It was entertainment. It was here the bear-fishing took place, and gave me a reason to leave the camp.

* * *

They began calling me "Buckaroo", the result of me saying I liked the movie *Buckaroo Banzai*. It was the only movie of the past decade we'd seen in common and I felt I had to like something they liked. I couldn't believe I let them call me that in front of the other men, and how, worse still, they smirked when they said it. It was as if, in some comic nightmare, I'd fallen below them in the human pecking order.

In a sense that was true. No evidence said otherwise. I considered myself through their eyes: like them I was a lowly chokerman, but one with less experience. Second, I had no friends. They had each other. In a sense, they had condescended to befriend me. Third, by their standards, compared to them I wasn't funny or witty at all. Would they have laughed if I told them that for me to stoop to their wit would feel like a self-lobotomy?

But last, and most damning, like them I had no woman. That I'd had one didn't matter—I'd been stupid enough to let someone steal her. In their eyes, "no woman" was the reason I stayed here on weekends.

What other reason could there be? Who in his right mind would stay when there was a woman in town, willing? I came to see how they idolized every other man in camp, simply because he left on weekends, meaning he had a woman. Give 'er one for me, they'd shout at the tailgate of a city-bound pickup. If you had a woman, you got home

Friday afternoon and you screwed as much as you wanted;
by Sunday afternoon you'd had enough, so you drove back.
I think they saw the invention of the weekend, and by
extension the calendar itself, as a creation shaped by the
number of times they imagined you could screw without
stopping.

Chip and Dale would joke slyly about those few who
weren't sexed out by Sunday and left Vancouver at four on
Monday morning, pulling up just in time for the shift. Phil's
pecker's still wet, they'd jive, and elbow, admiration on
their faces. It wasn't so much jealousy as awe. I came to
realize that these boys were not only mean nerds, but mean
nerd virgins.

Some sympathy crept into my view of them. Their
nerdy ugliness kept them virgins, their virginity made them
mean, and their meanness made them uglier still. I came to
understand their self-contempt, as well as their contempt
for me.

So, it was Buckaroo, with a smirk.

* * *

The dump was in a small clearing, near enough to the
cookhouse for convenience, far enough away for the smell.
It was a careless mound of stinking cans and cartons and
slop, paradise for bears.

There were grizzlies in the upper valley, but the
dump bears were black bears, not so dangerous. Though
there were stories of the odd treed logger, it was garbage the
bears lusted after. Still, I usually went after dinner when it
was likely I wouldn't be alone. Even camp veterans would
go to see the bears, some of which had names. There was the
big sow, Judy (after someone's ex-wife), a wiry old male,
Trudeau (from the familiar way these two swatted each

other it appeared they were mates), and a middle-sized bear, Cubbie (Cubbie sure's bigged up, I heard someone say). These three owned the dump, and chased any other bears away.

Weekends Chip and Dale and I would go to the dump at least twice a day, detouring in that direction without anyone saying a word. We'd watch them decently for a time, then Chip or Dale would start yelling or throwing things or making sudden movements to get them thundering off into the bush. Once when Dale lunged at them yelling, a roar exploded in Cubbie's stomach and he came. Only a few steps, but the roar had our hair on end, and those steps showed us his speed. Since that time, whenever Chip or Dale started acting up, I'd feign boredom and make to leave. They always followed. They could call me asshole all they wanted, but the invisible pecking order was the strongest. By letting them know they weren't all that interesting to him, Buckaroo could pretty much get his way.

* * *

Chip, Dale and I were at the dump, watching. A new bear was hurriedly foraging, as yet unchased. Dale lifted a pretend gun, sighted along it and pulled a pretend trigger. A kid's gunshot sound issued from his mouth, along with a bit of spittle. His voice fell to its sage tone.

"Those," Dale said slowly, "are . . . big . . . animals."

"Don't tell no one," Chip leaned over and whispered, though it was Sunday and no one but Dale was within fifty miles, "but the head we got on the pole, his name was Gretzky."

Dale got mad at Chip for telling me this. I gathered from what followed that some of the men hadn't taken lightly to them shooting Gretzky. One had threatened to report them for poaching.

"Fuckin environmentlatist," Dale muttered.

"It's okay," I said, "I won't report you."

"Better fuckin not," said Dale.

But the bear-fishing escapade was spawned then, when Kruger walked into the clearing, all geared up for fishing, on his way to the river. I liked Kruger, a man of few words, most of them dryly funny. I might have befriended him had I intended to stay.

Kruger stood beside us. He was almost fat, and wore a hat with hooks and spinners in it.

"What are those?" He pointed to the bears. "Those trout?"

Dale's mouth dropped and he was about to yell at Kruger but then he saw it was a joke. Still, he didn't smile.

"Some size to 'em too," Kruger said. He tied the largest spinner onto his leader. "Think they'll go for a Lucky Lunch?"

The distance was deceptive. I doubt Kruger thought he'd get that close because he jumped as high as the rest of us when his lure sailed out and grazed Trudeau's hind foot. Trudeau didn't do much but glance down, but we took off through the trees laughing and whooping like kids.

Kruger went fishing. Chip and Dale, still whooping, wondered where they could get rods and reels, and what the prize would be for the first one to snag a bear.

* * *

Talking to Rose on the phone I heard myself say, "As I told Chip and Dale the other day. . . ." I stopped short, stunned that these two were now a significant part of my life. How simple a life could get! How fast a life could de-evolve.

More and more I'd catch myself actually trying to

impress them. Usually it was harmless stuff, titbits of analysis, such as why certain trees exploded in certain forest fires. Or that tree planters were hired not so the company could make more money down the road (capitalists didn't think in terms of half-centuries) but to satisfy the Green lobby. Such explanations were usually offered to end one of their stupid arguments. Still, I felt a bit of pride during the silence that followed.

Once I tried to impress them with Rose. They were talking about how sexy John Stoat's wife was.

"But it's trouble goin' with a real good-looking woman," I said. "They can be *too* good-looking."

They watched me, hungry as hell for knowledge of this sort.

"Because other men start sniffing her tail. I found this out the hard way." I was nodding my head, but horrified at what I was doing.

Chip and Dale only nodded their heads back. I think it was a kind of bragging too exotic for them to mock.

* * *

They held the first bear-fishing contest after shift so the men could watch. They advertised it all day. A dozen men did come, standing around in dirty shirts and suspendered jeans, tired and edgy for a shower and dinner. Half left before the first cast because Chip and Dale were being such assholes.

Dressed up like clown fishermen (Chip wore a Bullwinkle hat, with shiny lures dangling the length of his antlers), they joked and fought over who'd fuckin go first, generally acting like a Chip and Dale amplified and magnified and sped up. In their defence, they'd likely never been in the spotlight before and it went to their heads.

They flipped a coin and Dale went first.

"Get ready to run you guys. Gonna nail this sucker." Dale studied the bears. Cubbie was closest, his head half into a green garbage bag. "We shoulda brought a fuckin gun," he added. Then, sagely, "These . . . are . . . big . . . animals."

"C'mon. Do it," came a call from the men.

Dale stretched his arm back, the heavy lure hanging like a plumb bob, glinting in the sun. He looked over at Chip.

"Hooker's gonna be a fuckin blonde, man," he said loudly so everyone heard. The prize was a hooker. It had been my off-the-cuff joke, during their endless argument about what the prize should be. They'd leapt at the idea, excited as six-year-olds. I don't think they got the silly pun.

"With great big goddamn juicy—"

"Jesus, go!" someone yelled. "Go! Cast!"

The rod swung in a high arc. The lure flashed in the sun. There was a twang, and the lure took off at great speed over the trees, so far away we couldn't see or hear it come down.

Dale cursed his snapped line while Chip, of course, howled. More men left. Aware of his dwindling audience, Chip stepped up with his rod. He cocked his arm.

"You don't whip it, asshole, you toss. Mine's gonna be a fuckin blonde *black* chick!"

Chip swung his rod, the line snapped, his lure flew away.

Other attempts to bear-fish drew no audience except me. They wore no funny outfits, and as usual it was a case of nothing else to do. But one cast finally hit.

* * *

Friday, four o'clock, dust from fleeing cars, settling. This was the worst time, because after all the car noise the silence would fall so abruptly. The mountains would suddenly loom up and for a few minutes, no matter which way you looked, you were forced to see and feel yourself very clearly. During this time, too loud, Chip and Dale would always announce colourful weekend plans.

But today Dale kept eyeing the direction the cars had gone.

"Why," he asked, in his sage voice, but with less power, "do we stay weekends?"

"We're savin money, asshole," Chip offered kindly. "If we went to town we'd have to have an apartment."

"But all the *time*? We never have any *fun*. We're never *gonna* have any fun."

I sensed the crucial word here was "women", not "fun".

"Yeah right, let's go and rent a luxury apartment to just live in for eight days a month then."

Dale paused, thinking.

"You know what we are? We're the—the foreign legion." You could see his mind ticking over. "We're—who's that guy, that skunk? We're Peppy L Pew."

"Who?"

"That skunk in the cartoon that tries to grab chicks but they take off because he stinks. That's us, man."

"Yeah right. *I'm* shootin some pool. *You're* an idiot."

Chip walked off looking mad. I heard him mumble, the guy's a goof. Dale was staying put, so I caught up to Chip.

"You know where the guy has to buy his glasses?" Chip asked without looking at me. "He has to buy his glasses in the kid section for fucksakes, because his head's so small."

Chip was sneering, but he looked immeasurably sad.

* * *

The next week I took to bed. I think it was a case of me wanting to milk things a little, go a little crazy. I think I wanted word to reach Rose. I wanted rumours of rage and illness.

That's what I think I wanted, but it felt like depression. I'd been toying with the idea of going home. Back to her. She'd let me keep my pride by suggesting I come back on my own terms. She even suggested that if I chose to pursue my own brief affair she'd turn her back.

I think it was this reasonableness I found depressing. She called her affair with Kovic "juvenile", using the word to explain why it ended. I wanted to tell her she was wrong, she had done it in the first place because it *was* juvenile. Juvenile: crazy leaps of faith, sex blind to reason. So unscientific: a heart grasping like a clenched fist.

My third day in bed, Chip and Dale came in, trying to save my bacon.

"It's not like I got an in with the boss," said Chip, and Dale giggled at this non-joke. "But layoffs are close. Better get up." He widened his eyes at the dire nature of his news.

"Holidays are over. Seniority's back," he explained further.

I still didn't respond.

"An' it's steak night tonight," said Dale.

"They bring him one anyway, asshole," Chip corrected him.

The thought of steak night repelled me. On steak night everyone was quieter as they waited. They could smell the good meat coming. Then the liquid crackling sound of chewing. But what I disliked most about steak night was what hung in the air: the gratefulness of hard-working beasts who thought they'd been given a gift.

"So if you don't get out of that bed you're gone," Dale said from the side of his face as they left. "You ain't union yet."

I lay back and considered. As if this job meant bird snot (that week's expression) in the first place. This job: work, work, stupid work. Aside from that, loneliness. And two crummy boys who disgusted me.

So why hadn't I gone home already? Why did I stay?

Because it was so easy here. You were fed and told what to do. You lost yourself in work. You even lost yourself in Chip and Dale's sour friendship.

So easily satisfied, we are so easily damned.

Afraid of being fired, and afraid of what waited for me at home, I got out of bed. And I might have stayed on at the camp a lot longer had it not been for what happened that afternoon. There was a kind of purity in what happened with Chip and the bear, a kind of clarity that helps you decide things.

* * *

They stashed a rod at the edge of the clearing to use when the urge hit. The bears no longer ran from this game. Chip and Dale were half-hearted in their casting, and in their descriptions of what the hooker would look like.

I caught up with them on their way to the dump.

"Well, buckaroo gets outta fuckin bed," Chip smirked, by way of greeting me.

"'Cause it's steak night probbly," argued Dale.

We reached the clearing, and when Chip announced that he was going first Dale didn't protest. Maybe it was this relaxed mood that helped Chip's cast.

The lure, a red and white spoon called a Daredevil, sailed up and seemed to hang in the sky, over the mound of garbage. The lure must have come down with a lot of speed and weight, because when they shot Cubbie to get him off Chip, they found one of the treble hooks embedded a quarter-inch deep in bone, right between the eyes.

It was actually funny how it happened. Cubbie got hooked in the face and fled from us, into the trees. Shocked, Chip found himself holding a rod, not sport fishing but bear-fishing, line shrieking off the reel. We were all stunned. Then Chip whooped. Then we all whooped. Chip hung on.

It probably lasted only a few seconds. What happened was that Cubbie did a U-turn around a tree and came back at us. But since the line kept pulling out of the reel, it felt to Chip like a bear still fleeing.

Brave and cool now, Chip had just turned to Dale when the bear came charging out.

"My hooker's gonna be. . . ."

I guess it was our head start that singled Chip out and did him in.

No man has a chance against such a big animal. I turned my head once and saw some of it. It reminded me of the quick pure rage of a dog fight, except this dog was ten times bigger and shaggy and roaring.

The roaring is unearthly.

And it seems a little unfair that such a big thing can move so fast you can hardly see it. Quick as jealousy or any of those other big ones. Chip was like its toy.

HEAVEN ON EARTH

Lucy didn't see it till almost noon. There were hints, small and large, but the morning's odd edge she took to be the result of drinking too much retsina the night before. A Saturday night. Her thirty-fifth birthday, with two loud girlfriends. A Greek waiter had tried to pick her up.

She got her first hint while riding the elevator down. Lucy was confused and bedraggled, had arisen only minutes before to pull on quick and sloppy clothes, and was on a mission to the corner store for her hangover cure: chocolate milk. She had not even had her morning pee.

A fat old woman rode with her. She carried a ridiculous large basket, had bunned hair, a puffy white face and mean raisin eyes. Lucy had seen her many times; she always got on at the fifth floor. This morning, to Lucy's surprise, the woman spoke to her. She sounded German or Swedish.

"Excuse me. My name is Mrs. Brink. I am sad we have never once talked." The woman stared not at Lucy's face but somewhere around her chest. Her raisin eyes were glazed, her face expressionless. "You must tell me your name. It is sad that we have never talked. And I must tell you now—I am not pleased with your hair style."

If Lucy had not been in pain she might have said something rude. But she gave the woman her name, nodded at what she was saying now (something embarrassing about a cyst) and otherwise endured the most horrible elevator ride she'd ever had. She ran, or perhaps it was just a fast dragging of feet, to her chocolate-milk store.

On her way back to her building, greedily tilting the carton dry, Lucy was stopped by a man in a suit and tie. He was her age and not bad looking. He said to her, "I don't desire you. I used to be on the Canadian national volleyball team. Perhaps if you dressed differently." The man was smiling politely.

Lucy took a long shower. She tried humming a song, an old Beatles thing, but could not. Two rude eccentrics in a row! She shook her head and winced again at the insults, then knuckled her scalp hard with shampoo. The two encounters died the fuzzy death of bad dreams.

She decided to treat herself to a leisurely walk downtown, perhaps buy some record albums. She'd browse in the import store again, the racks of *outré*, new wave bands. Lucy liked the store. Though the clientele were younger, and almost threatening in their leather, their calculated pins and rags, their pastel hair, she didn't feel uncomfortable. Her baggy shirt and punk-like jacket were a kind of ticket in, as was her haircut, a ducktail and modest crest with a touch of red dye. She wasn't sneered at in punk record stores, nor was she stared at in the bank where she worked. Lucy loved being able to straddle two worlds.

She went out into the street. Hints were now everywhere.

A block from her building she came upon two men who looked ready to fight. Clad in tennis togs, they had dropped their racquets and bags on the grass, and a short squat man had backed a taller one up against a building wall.

"No, I want you to hit *me*," the short antagonist was yelling.

So Lucy was relieved to see they were just acting out some kind of loud Abbott and Costello joke. But then she wasn't so sure. The short man looked desperate. In fact he was crying. She'd never seen actors this good.

"You hit *me* first, goddammit. Please!" the short man yelled still, his voice breaking.

"No. I can't. And it doesn't make sense," the tall man said. He too was upset but his voice was full of sympathy. "*I* seduced your wife, Bob. You shouldn't be talking at all, you should be trying to beat me up. Bob! You have emotional grounds for *murder* here."

"But goddammit!" short Bob was bawling openly now, "I want to be *hit!*"

Giving the two men a wide berth, Lucy broke into a half-run and didn't slow up until she reached Denman Street. The neighbourhood was certainly full of crazies these days. Perhaps it was a full moon. Whatever. Today felt undeniably out of whack. She should have stayed in bed with her hangover.

But Lucy had seen nothing yet. She turned the corner onto Denman, and the street was alive with them.

A woman walked toward her. A voluptuous redhead. There was something wrong with her, Lucy saw. It took her a good two seconds to realize the woman had no top on, no bra either. Her breasts were huge and aggressive, and bounced profoundly; the woman was taking wide confident strides, beaming ear to ear and staring into people's faces.

Lucy was into her third second of gaping when she was scraped on the face by a boot, the ugly black kind with the six inch corrective sole. In it was a foot, attached to the foot was man, a cripple. He was being carried down the sidewalk by three men and a woman. The crippled man's face was pinched by years of loneliness and fear. He was shouting.

"Put me down! Don't help me any more! I want to hate you!"

His bearers' voices were soothing and kind. "We can't," they told him, simply. They wore identical faces, slight smiles fixed on them, resembling a row of clams.

Someone else was staring into Lucy's face. A fat teenage boy. He looked concerned.

"Are you okay? That shoe left a black mark there on your cheek. Here, let me wipe it off." The boy was wetting his finger in his mouth. Lucy began to walk away, backwards. "Well, all right," the boy said, not following, "but you should wash it off. And most of your makeup too. You wear way too much makeup. Rouge. Old ladies do that. It's really ugly."

Lucy ran up an alley. After two blocks she could no longer hear street noise or see any people. She stopped and brought her hands to her face, and looked up at the sky between the buildings. A sunny blue-sky day. She was on the verge of crying. What was going on? Such a devilish circus of people. Such . . . *talk.* Such wide open eyes, eyes coated with such awful sincerity.

Lucy took long breaths. She'd never been insane before—was this what it was like? No, she decided she was sane. Or, at least, the same. No, the oddness of the day was not her private oddness.

She found herself halfway to the record store. She'd go there. It was in a quieter area of the city. She'd walk the side streets, keeping an eye out for people she could avoid by turning quick corners. By the time she'd covered three blocks she felt better, having decided that the city was to blame, that this damn west coast had pushed one too many people into one too many encounter groups, that the urban sink syndrome had at last driven everyone over some kind of edge. She would move to the suburbs and buy a car.

Lucy passed but one person on her zigzag walk through the side streets. The man reminded her of her father. He looked chronically sheepish, but his face had been conquered by sincerity-glazed eyes. He told her: "You would find me wise, and I *will* sleep with you if you let me, but I'd rather sleep with a young girl. A very young girl, twelve. . ."

"Shut up! Please just shut up!" Lucy was running now and the man called after her, his voice gaining volume as Lucy gained distance.

" . . . or even eleven, with a smooth face. She would be wearing a little lipstick but she wouldn't need to. She won't have shaved her armpits yet and her pubic hair would just be beginning to. . . ."

No one had spoken to her. No one was staring at her. Lucy stayed carefully apart, keeping her head low to the racks of records, changing aisles if anyone came too close. She found herself browsing through The Fixx and The Furs, and overhearing what a boy with orange hair was telling his girlfriend: " . . . because you don't even understand the music. I've always thought your choice of albums pretentious. You only see surface style. You're not as smart as me. And your earrings. . . ."

The shop had a used record section in the basement. Lucy descended the stairs and, horrified, found herself face to face with a man coming up. His eyes were glazed, he was staring obscenely into hers, he was opening his mouth. Lucy's panic erupted to sudden inspiration. She found herself shouting at the man.

"I am psychotic! If you say one word I'll take out my knife again!"

It worked. And now she was alone in the basement. Alone with her safe and normal past: Beatles, Stones, Simon and Garfunkel, Joan Baez. She would stay down here, think on things, figure something out. She could use her knife threat if she had to.

Then Lucy saw she wasn't alone after all. A man was crouching in the corner reading the back of an album, a Grateful Dead album. That is, pretending to read. For he was stealing glances at her. Now he was openly staring.

"I'm psychotic . . . ," she started.

"Go away or . . . ," he said at the same time.

They stared at each other, and Lucy's heart leapt when she realized that the fear and hatred in his eyes mirrored her own feelings exactly. They said nothing for a moment. His look was now quizzical, as was hers.

"You're . . . normal," he said, finally.

"Oh thank God, thank God," she said, and then the day's hell burst forth. "Christ what's happening out there? What's going on? Why are people so . . . ?"

"I don't know," he said, getting to his feet, still eyeing the staircase furtively, a kicked-dog look. "I don't know. I got up this morning and my wife was . . . brutal to me. She said all sorts of things. She wants a divorce. I have bad breath. She called me a know-it-all. She wouldn't stop. And then . . . the *street*."

"I know. It's horrible. People are so. . . ."

"Honest."

Their plan was to leave together. He had a car. She told him about her knife ploy; he told her he'd already punched several people in the face. Using their combined threat they hurried out, avoiding fearsome honesty, save for Lucy being shouted at by two punks who told her she was too old to dress as she did, that her fear of age and wrinkles demonstrated an uncool fear of death, and that she should get out of their store and go back to the suburbs where she belonged.

They made it to the car, locked themselves in and

collapsed back into their seats. They decided to head for the countryside. Just drive, just drive and think about what to do next.

"I'm Lucy," she said, offering her hand.

"My name is . . . John," he said, shaking it.

Lucy knew by his voice he had lied. She was glad.

John pulled out into the traffic, which for a Sunday was very aggressive. Many drivers seemed to be going as fast as they had always wanted to. There were people throwing themselves off the sidewalks in front of cars. Some were old, but too slow. Lucy snapped on the radio. Sunday was golden oldies day. The music would be safe.

"Wait. I lied," John was saying now. "We're in this thing together. My real name is Brian. I don't know why I lied. I guess I was thinking about my wife. Because, well, we're alone and . . . well."

Brian's eyes were sincere. Lucy became instantly suspicious. But then, after a moment, not. For it was good, of course. It was only natural for him to give his real name.

"I'm glad you told me," Lucy said.

Brian's look became instantly suspicious.

For a time they couldn't speak to one another.

The radio announcer was introducing the Beatles' song "Norwegian Wood". The music began, but the announcer wouldn't stop talking. He fought the music, talking over it, saying something about how he'd always disliked the song, how the lyrics were whimsical and did not make good honest sense, how he hated most of the music he played, in fact, but needed his job; he had alimony to pay, he was hoping to start an affair with the new receptionist and he suspected she'd be expensive, he hoped she would have him, he was not very good looking, perhaps that was why he'd chosen radio. . . .

Mrs. Brink, the Swedish woman from Lucy's building, proved very quick for someone so old and fat, and Brian could not avoid her. Lucy recognized her the instant her puffy hateful face sank in front of the hood. Two mountainous thumps bounced the car. Brian slowed, then sped up.

"Good God!" Brian said.

Lucy said nothing. She knew what she'd seen: a woman honestly wanting to die.

"That was horrible!" Brian said next. His face was white.

"Yes," Lucy had to agree, but even as she did so she found herself descending, found herself suddenly at her core. It was a place of awful certainty, as familiar as her bones, a place of such dark truth she was not shocked to hear herself say: "No. No, I don't think that was horrible at all." Nor did she care that Brian was eyeing her sideways now, in helplessness and distrust; it would only make tonight easier, tonight when she would tell him she could honestly not sleep with him because he was in no way appealing, because his nostrils were immense, with too much hair in them, because his wife had been right about his breath, because he could simply not relate as a lover should, because she could never sleep with him even if he was the last man on earth, which he was.

THE WALK

September once again. Andy had been back only minutes and already he regretted it. He'd barely unpacked before old Mrs. Barastall invited him downstairs to be with her real family and watch her die. Why hadn't he just found an apartment this year, like everyone else? Even residence might have been better than this, especially now, especially with her dying right below.

Andy had no experience with death. When her son Roger the landlord left after giving him her invitation, after explaining about her being home from the hospital to die, the first thing he thought of was her chicken roll-ups. Old Mrs. Barastall cooked on Sunday nights, the only meals Andy looked forward to here, and chicken roll-ups were his favourite. They took her all day to make, but she "made everyone pay for them" (Roger's little joke about the way his mother complained) by calling people to the table ten minutes before actually serving them. She'd ladle out the tooth-picked, dripping folds of breast meat and always say, "These take so much darned time to do right, but they're worth it." From his seat to her left, Andy always agreed with her.

But now, up in his room, he felt guilty for thinking about chicken roll-ups before attaching any weight to her death.

Whenever he told friends he lived in a boarding house their first response was to peer skyward at an angle, attempting to picture what one was. Their second response was to ask, Why?

He didn't know why. The first year he'd been late getting to town for the start of term, didn't know any better in fact, and ended up answering the Barastalls' newspaper ad out of dizzy innocence. Just because Sandra showed him the room he felt obliged to say he would rent it. It hadn't registered at the time that he'd be eating with the family and watching TV with them and the old grandmother and all the rest of it. There was one other boarder, but he or she changed faces every few months. And soon there was only Andy, because in his second year they stopped renting the other room and moved old Mrs. Barastall down to it, telling her they didn't want her "tackling the stairs" at her age. Andy suspected another reason: as he helped them move her dresser downstairs, Andy saw Roger's wink and Sandra's little bottomslap that followed mention of the newly empty room beside them. At last they could make noise.

"I'm just an old boarder now," Mrs. Barastall said, not smiling. Everyone including Andy laughed politely, assuming, hoping, it was a joke. It was her moving day, and she wore a grey track suit.

"You own the place, Mom," Roger said back, smiling, to tell her his was something of a joke too.

"Doesn't mean a thing," the old lady replied. She was good for that expression at least once a day, and what exactly she meant by it was no clearer now than usual.

Somehow, Andy had never heard that boarding houses were archaic. In his third year, a potential girlfriend asked him if he lived there because he missed his family. He told her no, not bothering to fill her in on the tired details of having only a mother he'd not seen since he was nine. She asked, Why else would anyone live at a boarding house? Andy didn't know what to tell her. He said, "Meals. I hate to cook." But it wasn't that. He didn't care for Sandra's cooking very much at all.

Each year, with something like surprise he found he'd ended up here again. Here again eating Sandra's runny casseroles (and waiting for Sundays, and wishing Mrs. Barastall would cook more often). Here again listening to Sandra bicker with Roger, a navy man who was away a lot. Listening to Roger Junior, ten, bounce an eternity of balls in his room and taunt his older sister, May. Roger and Sandra also fought with May, who when Andy first came here was fourteen and shy and slow to bud, and looked younger than she was. But she began to bloom rapidly, and the family brawls really started "that night"—as they called it still—a couple of years ago when she came home with beer on her breath. Sandra's subsequent search through her purse uncovered not only a condom but, even more disturbing, a ceramic moon amulet on the back of which was etched, Coven of the White Witch.

From the yelling it was hard for Andy to tell what enraged Roger and Sandra more, the condom or the amulet. It didn't help their rage any when old Mrs. Barastall, who had been listening too, entered to interrupt the interrogation by saying that true witches weren't so bad, not at all in fact, especially white ones. She'd known a few in her time and.... Roger's hissed "Mother! Leave!" put an end to her story.

Maybe the worst part about the boarding house was having to sit beside old Mrs. Barastall, in front of the TV, with nothing to say. He thought he could smell her: under the waft of floral cheapness an ominous undertone of something a little sour. Andy joked to himself that Mrs.

Barastall was the only reason he did well in school, forced as he was away from Cheers and Twin Peaks to be alone in his room with his books.

In truth, because of the old woman he watched more TV than he ordinarily would have. For one, she seemed to like the same programs he did. But it was more that he found it hard to work by—harder than her own family did, in any case—without sitting down and watching a show with her. She was, in his opinion, too often left alone, especially after her cancer was diagnosed.

And now he was starting his fourth year here!

Friends would still ask how he could stand living "with, you know, other people around." They seemed to love being away from their families, and would speak with dread, only half joking, about a coming Christmas. Andy knew now that boarding houses were weird. He didn't know himself why he stayed. He didn't really like it, but he didn't really hate it.

He walked down the creaking back staircase to Mrs. Barastall's bedroom. "She says she wants to know how your summer went," was what Roger said when inviting him down, his look suggesting his mother shouldn't be believed. Roger was only forty or so—yet Andy could not feel friendly toward him. Roger always seemed stiff and severe, even with him, the other man of the house. Andy wondered if maybe it had to do with Roger being in the military, that he was somehow always on guard, always ready for war with other men. He reminded Andy of off-duty policemen he'd met.

Andy hesitated at Mrs. Barastall's door. He heard voices, and then silence as a reedy whisper asked what sounded like a question.

Oh, he dreaded this.

Not so much Mrs. Barastall herself, whom he got on with well enough. Over the years they'd developed a kind of rapport where it was tacitly agreed to say nothing even remotely controversial, thereby guaranteeing a comfortable sit at the TV. One should have a pleasant relationship with boarders, seemed her credo. Sometimes, though, she would break her own rule by sending him a sly glance after a risqué TV joke, surprising him. At times he wondered whether he knew this old woman at all. Once, after a silent hour of watching two pretty bad sitcoms in a row, she'd sighed and looked at him in such a way that their age difference vanished, and said, "I wonder if there's nothing better for us to do than watch this crap."

No, what Andy dreaded was entering into family intimacy. Family was where Mrs. Barastall tried to toss her weight around. But no one listened to her. That's what made the arguments worse. That's what started them, in fact: she got nowhere and grew frustrated. It was her frustration Andy hated. Her frustration made him hate the whole family.

He saw the process as clear as day. Old Mrs. Barastall would say something reasonable enough, something likely starting with "In my time" or "Not that you asked my opinion but". No one would pay much attention. Roger might raise his eyebrows but would keep on reading. Mrs. Barastall's next statement would come out harsher, quicker. Then an argument would start, Mrs. Barastall would make less sense and start condemning "this poisonous age" and refuse to listen to them now, and the whole room would fall to a bad silence and feuding.

And while Andy stayed as clean away as possible from these feuds, he couldn't help but notice, for instance, that when Roger was gone old Mrs. Barastall would complain to Sandra about the setting of the thermostat, or the taste of salt in the gravy. Because Mrs. Barastall was on a salt-free diet, Sandra considered this little complaint, tossed off with almost amiable chattiness, to be a huge accusation indeed. Andy actually thought it a macabre joke on the old lady's part, one that stung Sandra before she had a chance of getting it. Sometimes Andy thought that no one in the family knew old Mrs. Barastall very well at all. Not that the old lady helped much in this herself.

In any case it was clear a family war was being fought, a war typical for its muddiness and almost grotesque subtlety, but nonetheless a war, and Andy didn't like his role as foreign observer. They behaved a little better when he was around, but he could still hear the muffled explosions, and feel the concussion in his gut.

Only ten minutes after arriving today he'd heard Roger and Sandra in the hall. Sandra was crying.

"She . . . she accused me of withholding her pain pills. I couldn't believe she'd . . . how can she even think . . . ?"

"What did she actually say?" Roger asked.

"Well you know how she says things without really saying . . . I mean, I came with her pill and she looked at me and said, 'Do you think I don't need those any more?' What did she mean? I just can't stand. . . ."

Roger told her it was going to be difficult for a while, that his mother was afraid. Then he said curtly that Sandra wouldn't have to put up with it for long, which of course meant to say that his mother would die soon. The way he said it reminded Andy of the kind of double-edged comment the old lady herself could be so good at.

Andy eased Mrs. Barastall's door open and went quietly in.

Everyone was there. Roger sat on the bed edge, holding her hand, talking softly, something about the Kuwaiti desert. Sandra sat in a chair smiling habitually, staring at her own feet. May leaned against the footboard and looked up when Andy entered. She said "Hi" like a contemporary, like a friend, like a potential lover in fact, and then quickly looked down. Andy realized she'd be eighteen now.

In the corner, barely able to sit still, sat Roger Junior. He squeezed a tennis ball, alternating hand to hand, to build up his wrist strength. His eyes flicked to everything in the room except his grandmother. He looked scared to death. Mrs. Barastall made the painful turn to watch him from time to time, and her eyes were all-knowing and gentle.

"Andrew, good," Mrs. Barastall said, noticing him now.

There she was. Her curly hair had receded dramatically, and her shiny skull looked like an egg in a grey nest. Her eyes alone looked alive. They seemed to bear the weight of a life that had gotten heavy, much heavier than her frail body. Every movement, every thought even, looked wrested up from within through an intense effort of the eyes. They bulged. Or perhaps the flesh around them had ebbed.

She was smiling at him now.

"Look," she whispered. She flicked a finger at the new TV which sat on the dresser top behind him.

"Some night?" she whispered.

"Sure," said Andy. "Cheers is on tomorrow night." He hoped his voice sounded right and would somehow make this woman happy. He'd almost added, It's a date. But he sensed the code that dying built, and this code said he could be humorous but not frivolous. Unless you were family. Families forgave all.

"Did you know I have a stomach cancer?" Mrs. Barastall asked, her voice breaking out of the whisper into a sudden deepness, like a teenage boy's.

"Yes. I'm sorry."

"Me too, Andrew," she whispered, and the corners of her mouth lifted. She looked at him in the way that dissolved their ages again.

The Barastalls and Andy sat and talked. Nothing important was said. It seemed Roger tried to steer topics as far away as possible from the reason they had gathered. He tried to get his mother interested in Iraq again.

Andy grew impatient. Something here felt crucial, and he felt a sense of waste. They should be summing up her life. Someone should be asking huge things of old Mrs. Barastall. He wasn't sure what. Perhaps: What's it like? Are there periods of peace? What do you think is going to happen when you die? But it wasn't his place to ask anything like this. It occurred to Andy that he might be thinking these things only because he wasn't related. He didn't know what it was like to be related.

A sudden breeze lifted the drapes for a moment, and everyone save Mrs. Barastall turned to the sight. Sandra said, "Hmm, windy." May agreed. Because of the drapes Andy noticed the pictures on the walls, pictures of a woman he assumed was Mrs. Barastall. In several, looking twenty or so, she was wearing sporty white skirts and accepting tennis trophies. Another showed her on a beach surrounded by black men and women, some of whom had tattooed and scarred faces.

One significant thing was said when Mrs. Barastall herself asked May if she would please promise to finish a college degree. May promised, looking embarrassed, as if she had just taken part in something right out of a corny movie. At the same time she looked stricken by the knowledge that she had just made a promise she would not easily break.

"Can't I go shoot baskets now?" Roger Junior was

whining in whispers to his father.

He was told "in a while".

"C'mon! You said ten minutes and I—"

Roger had his son hard by the arm and stared down a warning. The boy wouldn't look at him and he began to struggle against his father's hold.

"C'mon, you said!" Roger Junior looked wildly helpless, and ready to scream and thrash.

"Roggie!" Sandra pleaded.

Then, a reedy "Please, I'd like . . . to go for a walk."

So attuned was everyone to Mrs. Barastall's whispered voice that it instantly stopped the commotion. Roger released his son's arm, looking relieved.

"Mother, you're too weak." He paused. "Why not . . . why not wait till you gain some strength?"

His mother gave him a look of disdain. Andy expected a fight now. Mrs. Barastall hated being lied to.

But she smiled.

"I'm seventy-six, Roger. And I would like to go for a walk." Her eyes had a glow, and self-surprise in them. They drifted ceiling-ward, as if picturing something.

"I'll just go get the wheelchair," said Sandra, smiling and getting up.

"No, dear," whispered Mrs. Barastall, "I want to walk."

Roger and Sandra looked at one another. Roger raised his eyebrows. Sandra sent him the tiniest shrug.

"Maybe we could open a window, Elena?" Sandra asked.

"Walk," the old woman said, and shook her head.

"Maybe after a little nap, Mom," offered Roger, though he watched his wife while saying it. Sandra was nodding hopefully.

"I would just like to go for a walk," Mrs. Barastall

repeated. She looked close to tears now, or a fight had she the strength.

To his dismay, she looked at Andy. Painful as it was to meet her eye, it would have been awful to look away. He knew exactly what she was trying to say to them. Horribly, no one else in her family seemed to.

"But Mom, I ... don't think you *can* walk," Roger told her softly. He looked ready to cry as well. He clearly did not like saying such words.

"But I ...," Mrs. Barastall began. A tear rolled onto her cheek.

"We can all ... well, help," Andy said suddenly. "One on each arm."

Roger and Sandra looked at each other again. Roger let out a long sigh.

"Would you like your pill first, Elena?" Sandra asked her. "I know it's a bit early, but...."

"No, dear. As I've told you, I don't think I need them any more." She tried a smile. "I want to ... enjoy this."

"But Mom," Roger stepped in even as Sandra was taking her by the arm, "you can hardly even turn over as it is. A pill...."

"It's okay," Sandra said in singsong then, not looking at her husband as she moved in to help her mother-in-law sit up, having finally understood what pride hadn't allowed the old woman to say, which was that she wanted to take a walk one last time.

It took a long time to get her on her feet and into slacks and a sweater. She wouldn't hear of wearing a bathrobe. Then socks and shoes. Absurdly, jogging shoes.

Roger Junior was about to explode from fidgeting, but the hurt of his father's hand had scared him into keeping still.

At last, taking two- or three-inch steps, each one

begun with a grimace and followed by a sigh, with a son at one armpit and a daughter-in-law at the other, Mrs. Barastall passed beyond her bedroom door.

She stopped, turned and whispered something in Roger's ear. Roger turned and said to his son, in a voice that broke, "Grammie says you can bounce a basketball as you walk with us."

They moved slowly down the street, so slowly that if watched from a block away they wouldn't have appeared to be moving at all. Mrs. Barastall's foot lifted, moved a bit forward, descended carefully, touched down and tested itself to bear weight. After a pause and several measured breaths, the other foot would begin the process.

During one such pause, Andy thought he heard her whisper, "To fly on one's feet." Then he wondered if instead she'd said, "To die on one's feet."

Mrs. Barastall often stopped altogether. Then she picked up her head to see where in the neighbourhood she stood. A particular house or tree would impart something to her and she would smile, but say nothing.

"Mrs. Gilroy has done well this year," she said almost a block from the boarding house, having noticed a healthy stand of late-blooming flowers. Then she directed her family's attention to the violet window trim of the next house. "Eccentric," she whispered.

With her they walked, in a tight pack, a son at one side and a daughter by marriage at the other, then a grandson and granddaughter, and a boarder at the house she owned. It somehow seemed to Andy that she owned the neighbourhood too. That because of her age, and her utter patience, and the way her eyes knew the hidden details of the place, she owned it in a way that went beyond property and such. Even the way the sun lit her up seemed to speak of this. It was easy to picture her as a girl here.

Mrs. Barastall paused at an overhanging branch. A single leaf at the very end of the branch had already changed colour, orange with dead brown. She brought her hand up and touched it. It fell.

"That one's me," she said, and smiled to let them know she was joking.

They continued to move with her. The pace had bothered everyone at first, but now they were accepting. Even Roger Junior's basketball bounced in a steady, almost contented rhythm. The old woman's complete lack of hurry, her perfect patience, made Andy think of the word royal. Watching her, he also thought of the word matriarch, and for the first time he felt he understood it. He wondered again if her own family really knew very much about her.

Mrs. Barastall turned right then and caught Andy looking. She smiled. Her eyes were quick, and very alive.

Andy didn't know why but, as soon as she resumed walking, he envisioned, fleetingly, another culture, a society that revered old people. He pictured a strange parade, in which Mrs. Barastall was carried high up on a bannered platform, on the backs of men about the age of her son. He pictured people of all ages lining the path as she passed before them, she the longest-lived of all. They were comforted at seeing her. At the end of the walk there would be rituals, and a feast.

Mrs. Barastall had stopped again, and Andy almost bumped her. She turned around to look at May, who had dropped a pace back to walk beside Andy. Her grandmother pointed a finger to indicate a house they approached.

"Doris," she whispered to May. "Doris Honey. She was a white witch. Lovely . . . sense of humour. And very kind to me."

Mrs. Barastall continued her walk. They followed her

almost imperceptible lead. A power, it looked like, radiated from her. It was clear in her face. Andy wondered if Roger was seeing it too, for her son had stopped talking and now just stared.

It was pride at being able to walk, pride at having lived well and long. It was pride at having lived at all. And at having such a family, and walking with them in such a neighbourhood. It was only natural that she should be proud. This was as colourful, as rich, as any elder's procession before it had been. It was rich because it carried her whole family. It was rich because they wore all their fear and love on their faces. It was colourful because one was a ten-year-old boy who cared little for this event, wanting only to go off and play his games—which was only right. It was colourful because here was her daughter-in-law who had never liked her but who liked her well enough now, just in time. And here was her granddaughter who had been drunk and who was no longer a virgin, who had such a future, whom today Mrs. Barastall had seen giving Andrew the boarder a sideways look that smacked of inevitability. So young, so ancient, so rich.

And here was her son, her son, holding her up, a part of her own flesh that would keep carrying her long after her old body was gone.

It was easy, it was no effort whatsoever for her to pull all of this behind her in a procession and show it off to the world, because it was now so ripe, because it had become her body and because she regretted none of it.

Mrs. Barastall was not at all surprised to see the good way the sun began to shine at that moment. Or that so many friends and neighbours who had been looking from their windows were now coming out of their houses and beginning to line the streets, waving to her, with delight and welcome. So many of them she had not seen in years.

THE GREEN HOUSE

We were walking by the house the day it got painted. All we knew was that the Ditchburns had moved. I was fourteen, my four friends roughly that. We watched the new owners walk in and out pointing at things, proud and nervous. These owners seemed newer and more nervous than most. Some relative or suchlike stood high up a ladder rolling bright green paint under the eaves, a sharp, aggressive green that said nothing of trees or grass but rather some bad chemical. We knew the painter was one of them because he traded shouts with the wife in the same language. She was heavy, absurdly kerchiefed and for too farm-like to fit in with our moms, or this our neighbourhood. Her shouts sounded, as Mike Evers put it, "like a dog trying to bark in human."

Only during the trial did I learn they were Russian.

"Who'd want a house that shitty colour?" This was me talking. Someone said retards, someone said pimps. Out of sight, we exploded into guttural barks, Chinese screams and spews of anything foreign and stupid that came to mind. It sounded so lunatic I doubt if the woman had any inkling such noise was our version of her. But so it began.

Every neighbourhood has a Green House. Sometimes it's red, sometimes purple, sometimes mauve with canary yellow around the windows. They're all the same. Even kids know a Green House when they see one. Neighbours talk behind the backs of Green House owners and avoid them. The clothes they wear often show they're from a Green House as well. They send their kids to school in awful shirts. One imagines they're well-meaning and friendly, probably overly so. You'd lend them a cup of sugar if they ever came to your door and asked, and they'd bring the cup back promptly, smiling too much.

Nothing excuses a Green House. And if neighbours—who were our parents, after all—felt right to groan and sneer at one in front of us, that was enough reason for us kids to show the Green House no mercy at all.

We started innocently. That spring we hardly noticed them, so busy were we with school and baseball, and a new thing—stunned excitement about girls. But we passed the Green House each day after school. Someone would look up and say, God-look-at-that-fuckin-house, and we might shout in tongues again or make up stories. How they were inside right now eating mice and cabbage, or screwing shyly through a hole in a sheet, or sponging their armpits at a handpump they'd had installed in their living room. We called them the Gooks.

Sometimes both Gooks would be out in their new yard raking and pruning. They looked almost normal, in fact more boring than normal, though oddness was certainly there if you looked for it, which we did. She, again, had the dumbness and square body of a peasant in *National Geographic*. He was too thin and moved too quickly with his shears. Hair black and full, a bushy moustache, and yet a very wrinkled face. I guessed he'd been sick, though I didn't say so. His clothes suited neither these suburbs nor an office. I could think of no other word to describe his clothes than "communist". Assorted supercilious mothers who saw him during their shopping runs whispered that he didn't have a job.

With his shears and fast loamy hands, Mr. Gook was the gardener, while Mrs. Gook was the labourer, with her apt body, her hoes and baskets. And as the spring climbed to summer their garden became a remarkable thing. Flowers, roses, blooms of all colours grew against each wall of the house and out into the yard. These blooms were not only a childish and gaudy ramble, it all clashed against the chemical green.

My parents had been calling them "the immigrants", and now they took to calling their house "that toybox".

Walking to the park one evening (to sample some valium from the Everses' medicine chest) we witnessed the Gooks hosting a barbecue party in their front yard. None of us had ever seen a barbecue in a front yard, exposed like that to the street. Passing not twenty feet from what looked like huge sausage sizzling on a brand new grill, we were so instinctively embarrassed at this show of uncool we had to put our heads down. But worst of all was the party itself. We'd been raised on a version of barbecue where same-looking couples, summer dressed, held drinks and chatted. Sometimes kids would be included, perhaps a few captive lurking teenagers like us. The host might wear the latest funny apron. The women's drinks would be light-coloured and tinkle with ice; the men's darker in the glass, or a bottle of beer. The host would shout, all would move in to eat and that would be that.

The Gooks' party was an assortment of freaks, wonderful eye-food for us. Men in greasy T-shirts, big straighthaired silent women wearing starched bags. An old man in a wheelchair, smoking a massive curling pipe. Two fat old ladies—we couldn't believe this bounteous fuel for scornout—dressed head to toe in black, sitting away from the rest and not speaking. The few kids our age, one of whom waved to us but got nothing back, seemed of another world as well, their haircuts and clothes reminding us of a corny Walt Disney Ol'Yeller pack of hicks. The one who waved wore a jean jacket proclaiming Sgt. Pepper on the back, but without the jeans and sneakers required of it his hickness was all the more glaring. All the guests, the kids too, sloshed from great wicker jugs of red wine, the older men from bottles of vodka. A man my dad's age was weeping openly and thrashing his arms around. Others tried to calm him, but ended up thrashing their arms too. All this in a front yard.

Hours later, when too much lethargy pushed us from the park, we happened upon a dead squirrel. Dave MacIver toed it onto its back, then said, "*I* know." We got excited again for a few minutes, though no one moved very quickly. The plan was to put it on the Gooks' barbecue. We carried it with a forked stick and stood at the Gooks' gate. All was dark and quiet.

"But they might think it just fell dead off the roof," I said, always the thinker.

Al Cody snuck between two houses and came back with a toy boat, a bulbous red plastic tug with a smiling face comprising the deck and smokestack.

"Still not enough," Evers said, digging in his pocket. Out came a new dollar bill. A precious sacrifice at our age, but the perfect touch.

We crept down the walk to the Green House and then quickly back, stifling giggles. A squirrel, a happy-boat and a dollar bill sat on the grill, waiting for the Gooks in the morning.

We weren't bad kids. Except for Dave MacIver we were pretty good students, and athletic to boot. In the simple eyes of parents and principals, being a good sport excused you for any number of lousy deeds. But it is true that for a time our actions were guided by the darker hormones of adolescence. I'd like to say in our defence that though some of our shadier acts were public, and crude, we were no worse than the straight-A goof who goes home after school to his bedroom lab and burns flies in a beaker.

I did and still do blame Dave MacIver for much of what happened that Green House summer. He'd failed a grade or two, so was older than us. At fifteen MacIver looked like a mature Irish pug. His head was too large, his nose too small. A front tooth stayed chipped for years. It did occur to me that of us friends his family most resembled the Gooks—they were the poorest in Deep Cove, his parents had accents, his father shouted and drank and their small house stayed unpainted for as long as Dave's tooth stayed chipped—but I never put two and two together. Why we put up with him and even followed his lead I'm not sure. Likely because he was bigger and tougher, glamour for fourteen-year-old boys being identical to glamour for animals.

All the same, I didn't talk to Dave MacIver much after the summer. And when it came to naming names, his jumped off my tongue easily and without any guilt at all.

The week after our barbecue joke the Gooks had that haunted look. Mike Evers, who'd just seen a movie, said they looked like Italians who got a dead fish in the mail. It was probably because MacIver didn't get Mike's joke that he butted in and hissed out his latest plan. Yes, we'd all noticed those wicker wine jugs in their carport.

We began by making leisurely crank calls on weekend nights to see if they were out. It was the usual embarrassingly bad kid stuff: Hello, is your refrigerator running? etc. Al Cody put on a passable German accent and deep voice, pretending to be a government official who wanted to see their papers. When I took my turn I heard a raspy female voice say "Vot?" and then a babble away from the receiver. Clearly, they hadn't been understanding one silly word. Only MacIver took a different tack. Tense at the phone, his lips pulled back from his teeth, he'd yell at the top of his voice, *"Fuck off outta here."*

The next Saturday night they didn't answer for an hour so we wandered over. There in the empty carport sat the jugs, five of them, all in a neat squat row. We looked around, hopped the fence and hustled in. One of the jugs had a thermometer thing, fizzing with bubbles, stuck in its top. This MacIver plucked and broke casually under his foot. For the first time I had inklings. The look on his face scared me.

We ignored the fizzing jug and one nearly empty one, which those of us who could manage it pissed in. We lugged the other three out and over to the park, two of us taking turn as lookouts. Mike Evers dropped and broke one. I suspected even then that he did it on purpose, for he'd been the most squeamish about this prank, and the next week when we came to drink the wine he had a candy-ass excuse for not showing up.

But drink it we did. Most of it, in fact, between five of us, until later when two older guys shouldered in and hogged the rest. We sat around like calm professional drinkers and bragged about the deed, and as we got into it a bit we took turns trying to come up with the face that best showed the Gooks first tasting our piss, which had us falling off our logs and almost pissing ourselves. In a quieter moment I found myself remembering what I'd seen through the Gooks' kitchen window while we were in the carport. I wasn't sure what had struck me about the inside of the house. The pots and pans were somehow a little different. The colours and whatnot were nearly as crazy as the outside green. It all looked very clean. The one truly odd thing was a picture I could barely make out on the dining-room wall. It was of a giant human hand, very lifelike with the wrinkles and nails and the rest, but shooting out of the hand were these wonderful curling flames, some pink, others green. It was like a photograph, with great special effects. But besides all these colourful things there was an odd calm to the house, a stillness I found very likeable. Maybe it was what all empty houses had, I didn't know. Maybe it was my thief's adrenalin. But the peculiar stillness of that house felt welcoming. It made me like the Gooks. Naturally I said nothing about this to my friends, either in the carport or there at the drunken bonfire. They, and especially MacIver, didn't go in for such details.

The wine hit us hard all of a sudden. We were soon screaming and laughing, and before too long puking. I twisted an ankle badly, and the next morning I had no idea how. All of us felt hellish for days. Except for MacIver it was our first major hangover. And in that ragged, godless, nauseated state we found ourselves blaming the Gooks and saying things like, "Stupid house. Poison wine. Dumb bastards."

School was over now. Trying out an old skateboard, I was coasting empty-headed down the slight slope toward the Green House, and could see Mr. Gook sitting in his front yard in a chair. My feelings about them had levelled off: I knew it wasn't their wine but our own gulpings that had made us sick; since seeing into their house I felt I knew them a little; in general I felt sorry for their foreignness enough to want to let them be. In fact I hadn't even taken part in MacIver's latest prank, though it was one of my favourites, the dogshit on the doorstep thing. The idea was to collect fresh doggie do-do in a paper bag, stick it on their porch, ring the doorbell, light the bag on fire and run. With any luck you get to see a guy stamp a fire out and get shit on his slippers in the process. In any case, I heard it didn't go well at the Gooks'—the top of the bag had pretty well burned away and gone out by the time Mr. Gook came to the door. He just stopped and looked into the bag, scanned the area for faces, then slammed the door.

Skateboard noise made Mr. Gook look my way as I rolled up. I saw he'd been scribbling notes onto a bunch of papers and charts on his lap. Again, the back yard would have been the place for this sort of thing. But what the hell, I thought, and waved to him. He was looking right at me after all, and I felt magnanimous. He answered with a bored, somewhat superior lifting of a couple of fingers. Clearly a case of an adult condescending to a child.

His response surprised me, then made me angry. I don't know what I'd expected. Some kind of kowtowing. Something goofy or overly friendly. He was an immigrant and this was my neighbourhood. That he was allowed to live here because of my tolerance, my permission, was an absurd thought, but that was exactly how I felt, how we all felt.

He'd been studying my skateboard as if he'd never seen one before. Then he looked up to my face again. He studied that too. His eyes were remarkable things, the kind of silver-blue colour that somehow seems deep and empty and tends to pull you in. The eyes made the rest of his wrinkled face quite trivial. His gaze was simply matter-of-fact; one eyebrow was up a little. You could tell he gazed at things like this a thousand times a day. My anger fell to embarrassment, for his eyes made very clear that he was not only an adult, but an adult much smarter than me.

Perhaps they'd learned something, because they held the next barbecue in the back. This part of the property was surrounded by a fence plus lots of bushes and trees, so we hardly had to hide as we watched them.

It was a smaller gathering. The old man with the weird pipe sat across from one of the black widows. There was one couple the Gooks' age (it was the weeping man, who was sober this time) and the kid with the jean jacket. He wore sneakers, but the same hick pants. For the most part they sat around in chairs, sipped and talked in their dog-language. A whole chicken had been plopped spread-eagle on the grill. We knew there was no way they were going to get that chicken done without an electric spit. Mrs. Gook got up from time to time to turn the bird, but it kept rolling back onto one of its burned spots.

After five minutes we were bored. So Al Cody started things off by flicking a small pine cone into the yard. Every minute one of us would toss another, each cone more daring, landing closer and closer. I flicked a high wild one that arced and hung deliciously. We cringed and ducked when it ticked off the old man's shoulder. He turned and regarded some branches which weren't exactly overhead, but close enough to satisfy him. Next MacIver tossed a deliberate shot that fell into the barbecue. We hunched again and hissed, "Oh shit," while all heads turned to look. Some scanned the sky for passing birds. Mr. Gook was staring expressionless in our direction. But he didn't move, and soon they were talking again.

"Fuck it," Cody whispered, "let's spray and run." We each gathered a handful of cones and climbed carefully to our haunches. We checked to see if everyone was ready.

Cody signalled with a quick dip of head and then we were all grunting, throwing and leaping away. I'd seen MacIver scoop up the rock and now I heard the *crack* off a head and looking back saw Mrs. Gook go down on one knee. "*Ass*hole," I hissed as I sprinted. If anyone chased, they were no match for young men who knew, like rats know sewers, the secret veins of their neighbourhood.

I never told anyone, but several times over the following weeks I went by the Green House at night to stare in their carport window while they were asleep. Streetlight got in just enough to show me that festive interior, and in particular the flaming hand picture on the far wall. I always got that welcome feeling. I thought of the word "haven." The Gooks had made themselves a haven here.

I avoided the Green House for a while after the coning, but I couldn't help passing it one day as Mr. Gook was sitting out in his front yard. I meant to speed by, but couldn't resist watching him, bent and scribbling over his papers like that. I decided he was a scholar. Coming closer, I saw he marked a chart with coloured pencils. A photo album lay open on the lawn at his feet and he'd lean out to study it before marking his chart. What sort of work? Maybe he researched his relatives, his family tree. I imagined the chart to be an exotic scattering of countries, prison camps, holocausts. Squinting harder at the album I made out only abstract shapes and swirls of colour.

I'd slowed almost to a stop. I'm not sure why. Maybe it was the sight he made: under a perfect bright day, under a noble shade tree, this wise-looking man examined colourful things. We had just heard about the Greeks in school, and I had taken away with me an image of Socrates teaching in a place like this.

I waved. He should have seen it. Then I said hi, not

loud, but loud enough. He made no sign of hearing. So I hurried away embarrassed. How dare a Green House Gook be a snob. About to dismiss him as truly a dumb shit, I considered some options. Deafness, for one. Or more likely his scholarly concentration blinded him to all else. Or perhaps he rightly suspected me to be one of the tormenting hoodlums, and was doing me a kindness by turning the other cheek. I liked this last one.

I went along with the break-in for two reasons, and they were both good. I've thought a lot about it since, and I still think they were good. The first was a bit selfish—I wanted to check the house out more. The second was only good—I wanted to protect the house from Dave MacIver.

We were all so nervous. Even in the planning of it we fell to whispers, and any jokes we made came out stuttered and fake. No one really wanted to do it, but we all had to sound like we did. That's not true—MacIver was eager.

We knew now that Sunday was their night out. We gathered at the backyard fence. Besides MacIver and me, only Al Cody and Mike Evers had shown up. We watched Mr. rev the car until Mrs. appeared bearing a casserole and basket of bread. Off they went. We hopped the fence and, since it was the height of summer, we had our pick of half-open windows. We chose the breakfast nook.

MacIver went in first so I made sure I followed. We'd agreed not to break or steal anything big enough to bring us real trouble, but one look at MacIver there in the kitchen told me to watch him closely. Hunched, breathing hard and eyeing everything faster and faster as if he suddenly owned it all, he seemed an animal in some grim paradise.

I admit to feeling a sort of euphoria myself. It was wonderful in there, so cool, so dim, but with the bright colours standing out so sharply. I felt so full of oxygen I no longer had to breathe. Again, maybe this was the adrenalin of thieves in a dark new place. But I felt acquainted with this house. I felt like the host.

The last in, Mike Evers no sooner touched the floor and tasted the silence than he yelled, "They're here!" He climbed out and was gone, leaving just us three.

Following MacIver through the dining room, I stopped under the flaming hand. Dramatic up close, it *was* a photograph of a hand, surrounded by a rosy mist, with green flames curling out the fingertips.

On the other wall was a blow-up of Disneyland, Mrs. Gook arm in arm with Scrooge McDuck, her smile girlish as could be, her eyes half-closed and teary. Under the picture a bookcase held mostly dictionaries—English-Polish, English-French, English-Russian, English-Hebrew—and two books had a special place: *Welcome to Canada*, and *Canadian Fact Book*.

A fiercely whispered "Just *this*" made me turn to see MacIver take a knife in a jewelled scabbard off the mantel. More a sword than a knife, its curve made a quarter moon and reminded me of Oriental barbarians, who could slash with it, no stab. MacIver worked it into his belt. Before I could say a thing he whirled at me and stiffened up tall. Then said, "It's my *birthday*." That's all. We both knew it wasn't his birthday. His eyes were crazy.

I turned away, a host who'd lost control, as MacIver sprayed two decks of cards, a violent shower of squares, all around the room. This made Cody giggle like a girl. I decided I'd be the last one out, and clean up as best I could. But I couldn't stand here and watch.

I found the door downstairs. Descending to one immense basement room, lit only by dusk through two window wells, I flicked the switch. I saw right away that while the upstairs was hers, this was his. The walls had been finished with grey gyprock. The floor was still cement. The greyness was overpowering. Two walls displayed group portraits, his family, I decided. Stepping closer, I saw bearded men and sour women, in severe unsmiling rows. All were black and white, but from the looks of their clothes and the landscape, colour film wouldn't have added much. A wedding picture of the two of them hung in a special place, it too a drab grey. They looked frightened.

A third wall was hung with certificates and diplomas, most in foreign lettering but some not. The Indiana Center for Psychic Studies. The Parapsychology Institute of America. The Kirlian Institute Pioneer's Award. All to H.H. Karmapov.

The fourth wall was a giant grey curtain. I pulled it aside to find another room, a darkroom, in effect, for trays of developing fluids, chemicals and, in the middle, a monstrous black upside-down camera.

I felt like I'd walked into a rainbow. The walls were jammed with pictures of hands, feet, leaves, flowers, all emitting flames and swirls of violet, gold, lime and rose. One single finger tip, enlarged three feet square, revealed its whirlpool of fingerprint, from the centre of which issued a needle-thin ray of crimson.

I stared for I don't know how long before I saw the books, neat stacks and rows of *The Kirlian Annual* and *Truth and Myth* and *Kirlian Photography*. A single hardbound book had his name on the spine, just *Karmapov*. I thumbed through and saw in this book the same leaves, hands and feet that hung on the walls. One was a corpse's hand, with nothing surrounding it but a kind of muddy mist. I found the dining-room picture in one of the full-page feature shots.

I ran up the stairs. Mr. Karmapov was famous. Even MacIver might be amazed at this stuff. But in the kitchen I stopped, hearing their noises upstairs. A thud, wild laughter. At the foot of the stairs a bottle of perfume lay open, dripping its heavy sweetness into the air. I couldn't show them the downstairs. I wanted them out of here entirely, out of Mr. Karmapov's house.

In the upstairs bedroom they'd pulled out drawers, it looked like MacIver had slashed into some pillows, and Mr. Karmapov's ties were cut in half and scattered on the bed. They'd found some condoms and blown one up and tied it. The bathroom, where they were now, was strewn with Q-tips and toilet paper, and MacIver was lipsticking the mirror.

"Jesus, we gotta go, we been here an hour," I lied, trying to sound scared. I turned away in a hurry, took some fake pounding steps downstairs, then snuck back up and ducked into a guest room. In a minute Cody and MacIver followed, and descended. I started in the bedroom as quietly as I could, stuffing and putting back drawers, gathering snipped ties. I didn't know what to do. Write him a note, apologizing? Pay him back in secret? I thought of running home for my dad's ties. But I just stuffed all the damage into a pillowcase, to take.

I went to work in the bathroom, scooping, stuffing. I winced as something smashed downstairs, then more laughter. On the mirror and part of the wall MacIver had left a perfect image of himself: misspelled obscenities and one large swastika. I started on the swastika, remembering the Hebrew dictionary.

Then a muffled shout, some shuffling and banging. A car door closed, a kitchen door crashed.

"Vot? Vot?"

I don't know why I was running down to them, the Karmapovs, but running I was, down the stairs, glad the swastika was off at least, glad my pillowcase held most of the destruction. I may just have thought it, but I may in fact have yelled, "I've got it almost clean, it's almost clean."

I found them embracing in the kitchen, Mrs. Karmapov crooning and stroking her husband's head. They swayed. It was as if they'd done this before. I saw the broken mustard jar on the floor, and smeared ketchup. Cody had lost a sneaker climbing out the window. Mr. Karmapov was staring across at his flaming hand picture. It was covered with what looked like molasses.

He snarled when he came at me, and I could smell him. It was a smell of fear, and rage, and it was also a foreign smell. His magic blue eyes were so wide open it looked like he was seeing much more than me. Later, after the trial, I knew he was seeing other thieves, and brutal police, and it wasn't the first time he'd seen them.

He lurched. The clawed fist was meant for my face but halfway he pulled it in to grab his chest. He went hard to the floor but never stopped watching me, a half-lidded look so bled of colour it remains the worst thing I've seen. I had no idea what it meant until Mrs. Karmapov, her moans plaintive now, fell to him in the way that she did.

THE REVENGE OF RICHARD BRAUTIGAN

It started with Larkin bent over a sheet of paper at the table, trembling. So much rage sucked his chest concave, creating a den for itself there. One of Larkin's guilty secrets was that his rage rarely had a reason. Today it had a reason.

Last week on his twenty-first birthday he'd bought his first car ever, an Omni, for a thousand dollars, the exact amount of the cheque that had come in the mail from his parents. After insurance, all his money was gone. He had nothing left for rent or food.

Yesterday the car had lost its capacity for reverse, and could not dislodge itself from its parallel parking spot on the street. Today it had lost its talent for starting up at all.

In rage, having only to lift his head to see the hideous car framed in his basement apartment window, Larkin was composing a Brautigan to send to the man who had sold it to him.

A first line came. He scribbled it down. It dawned on him that he'd never used poetry as a tool before.

He did know that poets should not be dependent on things like cars. But all that was non-poetic in the world had conspired to see him in need of one.

Years of compromise in the name of art had forced him from bad job to bad job. Art had made him trade last year's present from his parents, a mountain bike, for an ancient computer. Now art had forced him out of the expensive city altogether, to this basement room in the outermost suburbs.

His city freebies had dried up. He'd even lost friends because of his "whiny scrounging"—once through a thin wall he had heard himself described thus. (The anguish, the gut-churning self-hate of hearing this, did produce a decent poem eventually.)

It had to do with this damn city. Nobody here avoided work any more. Larkin had watched street-poet friends turn scared and start believing that work was not only inevitable but somehow noble. Here Marxists worked at corporate gofer jobs, their only surviving statement being frayed collar, and lapel pin with red circle and diagonal line through something newly unjust.

When his ex-English prof offered him this room for a hundred a month (which Adam hadn't paid for two months now, sensing the room to be a gift and the mention of rent simply a face-saver), he had to take it. Free rent and a sympathetic landlord: this was the stuff poets must jump at.

In lieu of rent, and as a gesture of goodwill an English prof might appreciate, Adam had decided to dedicate "A Rocket in My Pocket" to him if *Quarry* did accept it. The poem was a bit street-smart for *Quarry*, but they'd had it six months now so it must be close.

It would be a stiff, prim world. These boxy suburbs were bad enough, but this landlord was a lord of boredom. How could smart people be so petty?

"I suspect you'll be typing," the landlord had "asked" after they made the deal.

"I have a word process—"

"I expect there to be no typing after ten. And no parties." The prof said all this with a shaking attempt at a pleasant smile, as if he were making normal, not fascist, conversation. Adam barely held back that he couldn't imagine anyone remotely interesting who'd want to visit this neighbourhood for the pursuit of entertainment.

In any case, now he lived in the middle of nowhere and needed a car. It too in the name of art. A street poet had to stay in touch with the street: with poets, with pace, with jive, with jangle. Adam also needed a car to have any chance at all with Greta.

In fact, during the test drive when the old guy said in his sleazy way, "Clean car like this, take your girlfriend anywhere in it," he'd pictured Greta in the passenger seat. He sensed Greta was the enlightened sort of good-looking woman who saw a car as a tool and didn't care what kind it was. And she might enjoy the absurdly hyperbolic name: Omni. All.

It seemed to run okay. When the old man shut up a moment Adam leaned brow-knit towards the dash, listening to the engine, pretending he knew which of those noises might mean trouble. Once he even said, "Hmmm," and tried to look concerned, suspecting that doubt voiced now would be a bargaining chip later.

It wasn't. He paid the advertised price, the full thousand, and when the car died days later, and he learned from a mechanic that the valves, carburetor and transmission would cost two thousand to fix, he phoned the old man. If you're not willing to fix it, Adam told him quite reasonably, then I'll take my money back with no hard feelings.

The old man seemed to be having trouble hearing. When Adam repeated himself, the man's chuckle, actually more of a guffaw, made Adam sweat. "Son, you bought a car from outta parking lot for a thousand bucks," he said, in a way that suggested change from lunch. He sounded in high humour. He added, "Young fellas buy cars like that to fix up themself. Do your homework, I'm not a jeezly babysitter." Then he hung up.

When he understood he'd be getting nothing back, there was a moment of yawning embarrassment before the rage came.

Not a letter but a poem, a Brautigan. For that was what Adam Larkin did best.

Bent over the table, a dial tone still echoing in his inner ear like the muse of irritation itself, Adam had only to look up at the car in the window to receive a new dose of rage.

He wrote:

You sleep nice at night? I know who you are.
I have sent my birds out
to grab the eaves and lift all the rooftops
in your neighbourhood, looking for you.
I am a large meat-eating negro
sitting in a nest of bones.

Adam scanned his Brautigan. Though more slapstick than subtle, it would do. He sealed it in an envelope, found the address on the bill of sale and walked the mile (jesus! walked!) to the post office.

Adam was young enough to consider every decision he made to be important. Big decisions he tended to think of in the third person, and in headlines: Adam Larkin Enrols in College. Or: Larkin Deems College Worthless, Quits. Or: Adam Larkin Dedicates Life to Poetry. Or: Snubbed by Journals, Larkin No Longer Seeks Audience.

This week the headline haunting the back of his skull read: Adam Larkin Will Accept Money from Parents One Last Time.

In recent years his requests had a putrid feel to them.

And he found he almost hated his parents for sending the money. To cash each cheque was to admit he was still a child. Worse yet, his smiling, New Age, freedom-forcing parents never once rebuked him or questioned his future plans. Willy and Edie themselves knew well the useless lifestyle from which his requests sprang, so there was no privacy, no way to lie. Willy and Edie, flower children made good, early buyers of cheap central coast land in B.C., pioneers in kelp farming, making a reality of the dreams which Adam could recall hearing as a kid, his parents and their friends talking endlessly, witlessly, over pot smoke and fruity tea long into the night.

His parents were professional idealists. Adam's middle name was Shine (pronounced Sheenay), Sanskrit for "peace". During his years in this city, Adam had told no one this ugly fact.

But it was Willy who had turned him on to poetry. Adam saw this to be the only influence either of his parents had had on him. He still recalled the night when, at fourteen, he had condescended to smoke pot with his parents and their friends. He had grown quickly bored with their serious looks and ironic word games so he launched into a cheerful description of how he and a friend had bashed a chipmunk against a wall that morning. How their stoned smiles quivered. He didn't bother telling them how fragile they all were, and that he had just made it up. But from that evening on, he made a point of emphasizing to his parents the fact of their different wave lengths.

Willy, though, had shown him poetry's magic simply by explaining how several words could give birth to an ocean of meaning. How the unspeakable could nearly be spoken. Of the many poets on his father's shelf, young Adam had taken to Richard Brautigan. Most other poets' word-salads about complex pain or poetry itself were boring or too hard to get. But Brautigan's stuff was short and sassy and funny. When Willy told him that Brautigan was "only a sixties poet" and that critics found him gimmicky and lightweight, Adam felt anger rise, though he didn't know why. When, only a few years later, he read that Brautigan had killed himself, the article hinting that lack of recognition was to blame, Adam was outraged.

On the long (jesus!) bus ride from the northern suburbs downtown to his Tuesday night poetry workshop, for a little warm-up Adam composed a second poem to the car thief, as he now called him. It had been four days. It was time.

The brake-happy bus driver made it hard to write, but his small moustache gave Adam a beginning. He ended up with this:

> Autobahn Hitler, you
> Omni monger,
> you slay the tender, you poison mercy,
> you sow the seed
> whose vine chokes with the fruit
> of man hating man.
> Lemon shyster prick.

It had turned out kind of classical—not much of a Brautigan—but this was maybe more suited to an old man.

At first it had ended with the "man hating man", but Adam thought this too light. The guy might not realize he was being pulverized. And though "lemon shyster prick" was crude, he liked the oblique pun of fruit/lemon, a kind of "bad cars are the root of all evil". And though he didn't care for the racist implications of shyster, a simple "lemon prick" would've been way too cryptic.

Folding it into the envelope he wondered, should he have said Omni in the poem? That is, maybe identified himself? Adam wondered how many Omnis the guy might have sold lately. But: Omni monger. Monger of all. That was pretty good.

Greta didn't walk in till the workshop was half over—though her walking in was so shy, so economical, so delicious. Her lateness had made Adam wrestle an irony: he had quit the workshop after the first class, returning to the second only after much reflection about the possible meaning of the look this Greta had given him as he was walking out. During the second class they had had eye contact, once rolling their eyes together in a shared mock of something Peel, the instructor, said. But then she'd left early.

And tonight she sat three seats in front of him and on the same side, making eye contact unlikely. Had she taken that seat on purpose? Was he only imagining this thing between them?

God, he hoped not, because he hated almost everything else about this class. Especially Peel, an arrogant dip who leeched precious Arts Council money to sit there on his desk top like an old hippie and say nothing worthwhile. The first night, when he had asked Peel what he thought of deconstructionalism (well, sure, maybe Adam had been trying to impress, but still), Peel had turned an arrogant dip's stare on him and said, "I look at words. I look at lines. Maybe once a week I look at an idea. But I never look at theories." Adam could feel his face redden. It was then that Greta turned around and rolled her eyes for him.

Tonight they discussed line breaks. And though the logic of line breaks intrigued Adam, he drifted in and out of attention, his gaze more or less fixed to the back of Greta's curly head. She didn't look his way once in half an hour.

Maybe he could conjure the guts to bump into her on the way out and suggest a coffee. Then what? Then they could wait together in the rain at the (jesus!) bus stop, then sip an embarrassed cup together, then enjoy a separate (jesus!) bus ride home.

Peel was onto the old idea that line breaks should follow the natural length of the breath. At one point Greta offered to the class, though talking to Peel the whole time, in a nervous but potentially lovely voice, "Would that maybe lead to a more conversational, and maybe a more accessible kind of poetry?"

Peel closed his eyes, nodded and then hissed, "Precisely," with explosive relief to it, as if she had just summed up everything he had been trying to get through to them for three weeks.

Adam discovered he hated them both.

He looked at the clock. A half-hour to go. He read what he had been almost unconsciously scribbling on his paper:

> *I bought a simple car from you and you simply*
> *weren't fair.*
> *Your lack of heart drains my heart.*
> *And when I'm heartless I make the world hurt.*
> *What's the price of this? I asked once in innocence*
> *when the subject was a car.*
> *What's the price of it now?*
> *You'll find out.*

Hmm, conversational. Yes, why not? Talking, ordinary talking. Communicating clearly in a poem. What a notion.

Though maybe it was a little sinister, in that the old guy might read a real threat, instead of what was meant, a more spiritual, "you get back what you give" sort of thing. But provoking a bit of fear might not be so bad. Adam still had faint hopes of an offer to fix the car.

The class ended. Peel went right to Greta, beating Adam by a good ten steps. As Adam passed them by, red in the face, she shot him a look he knew would keep him up that night wondering. It was a quick, concerned, hair-tossed look over her shoulder as he passed, then quickly back to Peel. The look said one of two impossibly different things. One: I think about you and I wanted to talk to you but damn I can't now because of this Peel and anyway I'm very shy and it's going to be up to you. Or, two: Oh god, there's the guy who's been staring at me and he's still staring, I hope he leaves me alone, he looks dangerously weird, he looks like he rides the back of a bus home to the suburbs.

Adam sipped his landlord's homemade wine, and stared at his car under the streetlight.

It still caught his eye a lot. His lone window framed the car too perfectly: if he had to look out his window at all, there it was. Nights it was even worse, when a streetlight glorified it from above. One tire had gone flat now and a second was halfway down. He imagined each tire hissing at him as it died in a long passing of sour gas.

In mere weeks rust had bubbled out in all sorts of places. Metal, rotting. The car was teaching him about the mutability of seemingly solid matter. But that was the only good thing it was doing. The man had to pay. This was serious now. Adam hadn't eaten for two days.

If he had to extract revenge with poetic pestering through the mail, so be it. It was working.

The man had phoned for him, twice, at the down-town place his name was last listed. Yesterday Adam had run into one of the guys he'd lived there with, Livingston, who told him a "car guy" had called.

"Really?" Adam asked him. "And?" He half hoped to hear something about repairs or being paid back.

"He started yelling at *me*," said Livingston, not pleased. He and Adam had never liked each other much. "When I convinced him I wasn't you, he told me to tell my— I'm quoting here—to tell my jeezly bastard friend to stop sending him jeezly fucking messages. He sounded old and stupid. I think he actually said 'jeezly space messages'. When he phoned the second time, all he said was, 'You warn him. You just warn him.'"

That was yesterday. Today Adam decided to pick up the pace of the attack. More poems, mailed in different-sized envelopes, so the thief would open them, not knowing.

Adam was amazed how fast this homemade wine was hitting him. It tasted so weak. Two days without food, perhaps. The headline, Poet Starves Awaiting Cheque from Parents, had been lurking ever since the first hunger pains.

There must have been a good thirty bottles of the stuff in the storeroom Adam passed on the way to his room. In three months he had gone through perhaps ten. Maybe twenty. In any case, a very visible dent in the supply. But the prof had said nothing, and Adam imagined him there upstairs smiling at the notion that he had living beneath him a Faulkner or Fitzgerald or Lowry, composing while inspired by purloined landlord wine.

Adam's thoughts turned to Richard Brautigan, also quite the boozer apparently. He tried to imagine this writer, so ripe with insight and twisted wit, in such despair that he would kill himself. Adam imagined him a gentle sort. His poems gave proof of that. They championed love over combat, the weak over the strong, the whimsical over the certain. One book's title, for instance, *The Revenge of the Lawn*, suggested the gathering rage of something weak and mundane and forgotten. It was a joke title, but still.

Sipping wine, Adam thought of his own revenge. Poetry was . . . was like a lawn, yes. Trampled and shit on. Poetry and lawns were forgotten by the world, and when they were remembered they were remembered as a chore. Or merely pretty. Poetry was thought to be a feeble thing, old lady stuff. Adam believed—jesus but he was getting a bit drunk now—that by invoking the spirit of good old dead Brautigan in this poetic crusade against injustice, against the hordes and cheaters and philistines, he was avenging all slighted poets, he was avenging poetry itself.

He decided to watch a bit of TV while he composed his next Brautigan. A little black-and-white set he'd found abandoned in dust next to the mousetraps and wine bottles. He staggered on his way to it now. Cheap wine, empty stomach, another lurking headline: Poet Drinks Self to Death in Suburbs. Maybe he could steal some crackers or something from a corner store. Starving Poet Thrown in Prison. The TV got only two stations, and Adam chose the old western over the news. Then, what the hell, he stumbled to the storeroom for another bottle. A switch to red, which was a little more like food. He didn't care for writing poetry while drunk, let alone while watching TV, but it did keep his hand in on the seedier side of letters.

The next morning, palms pressing temples, he read what he'd written. The duster had been corny, a John Wayne. Adam remembered being in a soused, ironic, almost friendly mood.

> *Weevil ass, dirt-lickin' skunk,*
> *Owl-hoot hombre of Dodge city,*
> *yah up an' rustled muh steer.*

Ah feel like a limpy fetch-dude
fer bein' taken so.
But yeeeeehah:
Ah'm down but ah ain't out.
Yah best be on the lookout,
tie yer balls up tight fer a shoot-out:
Slap leather!

It wasn't too impressive, as was usually the case with alcohol-inspired work. But the Omni was in fact a Dodge, and this lent an air of auspicious coincidence. Also, "limpy fetch-dude" would never have come to him from a sober muse. It was Brautiganesque. And it dawned on Adam in a spasm of oblique, hung-over inspiration, as from beyond the poet's grave, that Brautigan would have written "slap weather". To show the utter absurdity of combat, yes!

Adam changed the "l" to a "w", and into an envelope it went.

Adam missed poetry class because he had no bus fare, and spent the evening wondering if Greta missed him. In the week that followed he plucked cans of food from what appeared to be a bomb-shelter sort of emergency box hidden in his landlord's cellar storage. He hitched in the evening of the next class and managed to borrow ten bucks, from Livingston of all people, and now he sat in the classroom awaiting Greta's entrance, his stomach full of burger and fries. Not good poetry food—grease in the belly made him feel stupid.

The ten also gave him money for stamps, one of which went on an urgent letter to his parents (apparently his first letter had sounded too casual; they hadn't sent money yet). The other stamps were used on a backlog of poems to the car thief.

Greta finally arrived and sat down. Peel took this as a cue to announce to the class today's topic.

"Consider this," he said. "The written word is little more than the corpse of communication." Peel winked at Greta.

Adam saw it, an actual wink. Of all the unprofessional, uncool, grotesque, slimy ... Adam ran out of words. Sure, certainly he'd entertain the oh-so-original notion that language was imperfect. That there were events out there poetry couldn't capture. That body language, a loving gaze, a sneer, the Vulcan mind-meld for christsakes, could do a quicker, more subtle job than words. Jesus! Adam had seen the limitations of words when he decided to be a poet at fourteen!

His hand went up.

"So how do we write poetry without words?" Adam asked, when Peel nodded at him. Peel, the corpse of education.

Peel smiled. His half-closed eyes actually flicked down to see if Greta was watching him.

"You can do poetry on the stove. You can do poetry in the choice of shoes you wear. You can do poetry with the way you count out change to the Italian shopkeeper. You can do—"

"Write. I said how else do we *write* poetry."

Peel's smile grew wider as he shook his head as if to berate Adam for persisting with a very dumb question.

"Of *course* we all see that poetry is not life itself," Adam said. He was enjoying this. The strain on Peel's smile showed he was not used to dealing with poets who lived and died poetry. Adam had another phrase ready, one of his father's. "We *know* that poetry is a poor translation of experience, but. . . ."

"I'm talking about something else," said Peel. "I'm

not suggesting we translate anything at all." He said "translate" in the same spitting way a teenaged communist would say "bourgeois".

Peel paused to make everyone wait. Greta had spun around to stare at Adam. Her look was defiant. There was no doubting now she was in league with Peel.

"I'm talking about creating poetic experience," Peel said slowly, for stupid Adam's benefit, "not merely translating ordinary experience into poetry."

"Yes, you see," this was Greta talking at him now, the room taking on the quality of conspiracy, and religious conspiracy at that. "You see, we can live poetry. Our lives can be a poem." Her brow wrinkling up, she asked with concern, "Did you miss last class?"

Ah! That was it, last class must have been when Greta and her dupe Peel had taken control of a poetry workshop and changed it to a course on The Way of Happy-Face.

Adam got up. He felt quite calm. He had never done such a thing before, that is, exit a war zone under perfect control.

On his way out, he said simply, clearly, "This is silly."

And in walking out Adam somewhat proved their point. Hadn't their point been, simply, actions speak louder than words? Even as he left he could see the effects. His action had turned Peel's face to a mess of self-doubt, and Greta's happy-faced concern to ordinary anger. As for the class, its collective face appeared split over whether this workshop was indeed "silly" or not. Some seemed to want to follow Adam Larkin, street poet, out onto the street.

So it was ironic that Adam actually agreed with Peel and Greta, though no one knew it. In fact, what he'd meant by "this is silly" had less to do with what had been said than it did with his main reason for being there: Greta. Saying it, he'd meant it was silly for him to keep hanging around when Greta was so obviously cozied up with Peel.

No, he agreed completely. There existed a whole school of poetry that transcended the written word. You could do it with the voice, you could do it with the body. Life as art. It was the stuff of masters. It made people wake up, or worry, or rage.

Maybe he was just getting feeble and light-headed from lack of food again, but after striding so poetically out of that final class, it seemed that his life did turn into a poem. A raw sort of poem, one with bite to it.

Things got intensely poetic the next day at the post office. He did the walk weak with hunger but eager in knowing a special delivery letter was there. Opening it he found no cheque, just a note. They told him, in tones chatty and cheerful as ever, that they were quite bankrupt. Kelp had been a long fad. "Oh well," they concluded. "We'll send a bit of scratch if there's any left after the house sale goes through. But it looks like we bought at a bad time. So sell a poem! Just a joke. Edie and Willy."

The oddest thing about this was Adam's unexpected lifting of spirit as he walked home. The putrid feeling was gone. He actually felt, well, good about it all. He decided he loved his parents. He felt older, free. Hungry, but free.

Poetry flared again on the walk home when Adam decided to stop sending Brautigans to the car thief. This was poetic because mere seconds after his deciding to forgive and forget, here were two young men waiting beside his landlord's garage. "Larkin," one of them said, and when Adam turned to the voice, already flinching at the threat in it, they started punching.

Even while being punched, even with three teeth loosened from their perch in his skull, Adam was amazed how the excitement, the adrenalin, was a painkiller. It's Not

Hurting Much! came a sudden headline. The only thing that hurt was the kicks to the ribs, and only from the guy whose boots were a little pointed.

Suddenly they were finished. Through one eye, the one that wasn't staring into the grass, Adam watched their legs walking away, right past the Omni. He heard one of them say, perhaps as an afterthought, for it sounded like he didn't even bother turning his head, "Quit buggin' Dad you little fruitcake."

The clicking of their heels hadn't faded away before he felt embarrassed to be sprawled on his landlord's lawn, beaten up in broad daylight. Poets got beaten up in bars, not on suburban front lawns. He knew there would be blood on his shirt when he got up. He hoped his landlord was gone.

Rising to his elbows, moaning, Adam found himself thinking this: how effective their act, how pathetic his own words by comparison. He wondered what else they might do, considering the poetic time lapse caused by Canada Post. What would they make of the poems yet to arrive, one of which described their mother as a suicide who, fed up with her husband's heartlessness, jumped off a tall building, her body flattening on impact into a perfect replica of Italy, her homeland.

Adam stood watching himself in the mirror. He'd never had call to use the archaic word "wretched" before. One eye was shut. His upper lip was sticking out like—funny how this childhood word came out of nowhere—like some goober's. Hardly any discoloration yet, just grotesque swelling. He heard his landlord's car pull into the garage.

Three teeth hurt, and, if he took a step, his ribs. One funny part was that his last clean pair of pants kept sliding right off his now gaunt (he'd never used that word either) hips, and when he strapped on his belt it didn't work either until he punched two new holes in it.

Beaten Poet Cinches Belt. This headline and another—Pathetic Scene in Basement Apartment—entertained him as he winced while he cinched. He found he had a limp as well, which caused him to smirk into the mirror and whimper, "God bless us, every one," and laugh, which brought on sobering jabs of pain.

He didn't feel entertained for long. Things had gotten just a bit too stark. Hunger had ceased to be an experiment. And now he couldn't apply for a job looking like this.

Adam opened his door on his way up to ask his ex-prof for an emergency loan, when, in a new stanza to this odd poem, there stood the landlord himself at the door, hand up to knock.

His face was red. He wouldn't look Adam in the eye. Adam saw a shy man, a last-straw man, a man with the clipped breath and furtive eyes that spoke of worked-up nerve.

"I suspect a deal should be a deal," the prof blurted, too loud. "I must ask you for the rent. You have not paid once."

"Okay," Adam said.

The prof seemed startled by this easy agreement and he looked up. Adam could see his swelling bruises register on the landlord's face. He appeared angered by them, and driven to say more.

"It's my father's wine. You might have asked. I might have given you some. Now I might have to ask you to leave."

"Okay," Adam said. "Whatever." He pictured the dusty bottles. He remembered the mouse.

"And move that car. Today." The prof wouldn't look at Adam any more. "We'll just have to see," he added, in victory. Nodding once fiercely, he spun away and ran noiselessly up the stairs.

Adam sat in a chair for five minutes, in a sense composing. He heard the landlord's car leave the garage, asserting itself a bit more loudly than usual as it drove off into the dusk.

Adam went to the storeroom for the mouse. There it lay, caught in the prof's trap, not yet stiff. Adam pinched a wooden edge and picked the trap up. It looked like a clean mouse. Its fur glossy, the animal had somehow lived and died free of the dust. Adam lifted the bar and slipped it out. He felt its body, the movement of tiny bones in loose muscle, the syntax of fresh death.

It made him think of Richard Brautigan's last poem—suicide. Suicide was powerful work, no question. It made people sit up very straight. But, in the end, it was too ambiguous. There was the possibility of reading a whimper in it. Poetry was many things, but it was never a whimper.

And you couldn't go back and edit.

Up in the entryway Adam dropped the rodent into an inner chest pocket of his landlord's winter coat, a coat he wouldn't be using for another few months or so. A little poem for him.

In the garage he found lighter fluid and a box of old books, many of them poetry. He selected five for their fatness and soaked them. Poem number two would be more obvious, and over much sooner than the mouse. The Omni had a quarter-tank of gas in it, which might even explode. Some poems took on a style of their own.

An explosion, or creeping rot. Adam wondered which would prove the better piece of work.

OPERA OF THE ELK

After a week of knowing him, I began to play the gadfly with Douglas. A composer of music I didn't understand or much care to, he was educated, upright, and cultured to the point where snobbishness was a given. But he was Australian and loved beer, and was known to get raucous at times. So I thought he could stand some ordinary Canadian boorish pestering.

"You have a chance of ever making a living off your shit, Douglas?" I asked.

It was last call in the Banff Centre bar. Everyone else at our table had gone, and we had several beer apiece in front of us. It felt odd, the two of us occupying such opulence. Fireplaces, couches, art on three walls. The fourth wall was glass, and looked out over the pool.

"Probably about the same chance as you and your . . . shit," he said. He didn't look at me.

We were both in the same dire pot, considering the era. He composed classical, I wrote literary. Here in Banff we were both finishing off major projects: an opera, a novel. But Douglas was stuck. Friends said this had nothing to do with his wife. Almost finished, he couldn't finish. Something had dried up. His plight was well broadcast throughout the colony.

Douglas turned to me with an appraising look. We had never talked seriously before.

"When you write a novel," he asked, eyes bugging a bit, his whisper almost a hiss, "do you just sort of start, or do you have a structure? An idea with an ending, that sort of thing."

I explained I'd finished two novels. The first had had an idea with an ending, the second I'd simply started and pushed on with blindly. The third, the current one, was a hybrid, with a central idea so hazy it could use rupturing if the right surprise came along.

"Oh," he said. And then, "Christ! So which is best?"

I told Douglas I couldn't say, being a feeble critic of my own work. But I did say that writing without any end in mind was certainly scariest.

"If the book goes nowhere worthwhile," I explained without having to, "it can waste years of your life."

"Yes," he said. "Right." Then, the beer and his Aussiness taking over in a kind of fit, he screamed, "Christ!" in falsetto, and laughed. Douglas was unfortunate in that a severe angle of eyebrows made him look evil, though I don't think he was. A receding hairline gave him the height of forehead every genius was thought to have. His face turned red whenever he laughed painfully—which was the only way he laughed.

We went silent a while. Douglas hunkered down over his beer like any good lovesick Canadian. Then he asked me if I cared to hear about his opera. He'd been in these artist colonies enough times to know how horrible it was to just come out and talk about your own work. Some artists did this endlessly, usually the lesser ones—they talked work but rarely actually did it. But I said sure, indicating with my hand the beer on the table, the time we had to kill.

He told me his opera was inspired by a Beckett play, a depressing beast it sounded like to me, and that the opera had four major movements: Birth, Suffering, Old Age and Death. Before he'd written a note, Douglas had compiled fifty pages of structure: the keys of each movement and submovement, tempo, the counterpoints, where and why the oboe would overlay which violin, and a hundred other minutiae which flew so far over my head they were in no danger of colliding with the Banff mountains. He was into a rant now, and it was impolite of me to keep listening when I didn't understand. I interrupted with a guess.

"The structure's painted you into a corner?"

Douglas nodded slowly over his beer. He explained that the nature of formal music meant that with each note you selected, you cancelled infinite combinations that could have followed.

"I mean you can't just," he said quickly, "you can't just plop in a bunch of C-flat strings going niggle-niggle-niggle. *Christ!*" He guffawed and shook his head at the absurdity of the notion.

"Well, how the hell," I said, "do you write music suggesting 'Age' anyway? Who the hell would know? Who would know niggling C-flat strings were wrong for 'Age'?"

"The people who matter."

He said this so casually it was hard to feel insulted. I should have stopped here, my knowledge of music being at its limit, but I didn't.

"Maybe all the structure is boring in the end. Maybe people like surprises. Incongruity. Stuff that doesn't fit. Jazz if full of surp—"

The look he gave the word jazz burned both that style of music and my line of reasoning to instant ash.

"Well, what do you want?" I asked. "What do you think people want? Surprise or structure?"

Douglas said, "Structure," so quickly and with such certainty that I thought for a moment he must be right. He

added, "Life has *no* structure and it's crazy." He paused.
"And it hurts."

I nodded at that one. His look of certainty didn't fade.

"That's why people like art," said Douglas. "That's
why they like your fake stories, that's why they like TV and
that's why they like my opera."

I was going to add "all ten of them" to the opera part,
but didn't trust my sense of his humour. And, also well-
broadcast around the colony was news that a month ago,
back in Oz, his wife had left him, taking their child. He'd
received a letter. He'd been seen crying on the cafeteria
steps. But he'd stuck it out here with his opera, his art.
Though perhaps there was just no longer much reason to go
home.

"Life has enough surprises," he said. He looked at me
pointedly, making sure I knew what he was referring to.
"And I feel crippled by them."

I nodded, recalling a few bad surprises I'd had over
the years too. Their taste was still on the tongue, the homes
they'd hollowed out for themselves were still down there in
the gut.

"Art is structured chaos," Douglas said. He gulped
beer. Then added, "Most welcome."

"Lightning in a box," I offered, though I didn't really
want to agree yet.

"Thunder in a jar." He was smiling now. I could see
this helping, this airing of pain.

"Tempest in a teabag. Trauma in a test-tube."

"Haw-haw! *Christ!*"

Below, through the wall of glass, a lone woman
splashed, tiny in a corner of the pool, a huge aquamarine
vessel that hardly noticed her. Here, we two were jerking
around laughing, held up and shaped by straight-backed
chairs. We drank fizzing alcohol, contained in bottles.

Controlled chaos. You could prove any theory you wanted to here in this bar.

"So you're stuck," I said.

"What I've written so far has left me with extremely limited choices, and none excite me."

Again adding that I knew nothing about music, I offered that it might be the same in writing. I told him that in my current book I had Mary taking a hike in the deep woods, because the plot demanded a tryst with an old lover there. Mary was a city person, so I had to have her respond to being alone in the woods. But she had surprised me. Instead of a clichéd, timid appreciation of birds and pretty mushrooms and whatnot, Mary was repelled by what she saw: the dank rot, the diseased leaves, and bird cries that sounded only aggressive and hungry. She saw a limping rabbit, not long for this earth. She surprised me further when she realized that this view of nature was in fact an accurate one. It was the complete, fleshy version. It reflected all life, including her own. Then, meeting her lover, going at it in the twigs and dirt, she saw sex with the same eyes. None of this really fit my plans for the book, but it made it better.

"Anyway," I told Douglas, "even when you're just filling in the blanks of the structure you made, surprises have to happen. They're the best parts."

He sat nodding slowly, whether from agreement or boredom I didn't know. Artists really should not talk about their own work.

"But . . . Christ," he said. "But I have to . . . imitate something. I have to imitate sadness. Rage. The tempo of a heartbeat. You know?" He was serious but smiling. "The trickle of a tear? Plinking, dit-dit, on a white breast?"

He stopped. He stared off, and the falsetto "Christ" rang softly under his breath.

A young woman, saying, Sorry, it's the rules, told us to hurry and finish our beer. We guzzled. We talked of other things. Marriage. The hard truth of a child. Things I knew less about than music. Douglas cried briefly at one point, unembarrassed. He looked used to it now. We spoke of exchanging addresses, and I promised to make it down under to visit. When you're drunk I think you actually believe what you're saying.

"It's a crazy place," Douglas said, and he confirmed this with a look that was classically mischievous and indeed a little crazy.

"Maybe it's the island thing that does that," I added, and then couldn't resist, trying to sound wise, "an island is structure. People are bursting to get out. Off."

"Well, no they're not," Douglas said, and we both laughed.

Drunk, Leonard the painter thumped past our table and grunted at us without looking. Baby-faced Leonard was near forty and pale and puffy and on the verge of grotesque. His real name was Robert, but he wore Leonard Cohen clothes and, when he wasn't painting, did little except huddle up with women and try to whine his way into one of their rooms. He had no time for men.

Douglas and I were drunk now. We made motions of leaving. I felt I hadn't helped him at all. The presumption that I could help a classical composer compose didn't bother me—this wasn't just music, this was art stuff. Gut. Heart.

"Just go sit at your piano. Right now. I have some tequila. I'll give you some. Bang off some stuff." I was insistent, loud. "Doug—it'll fit. Shock fits. Shock 'em. Shock the fuck out of 'em."

"My god. Nest of gibberish! Cretinous *Chri...st!*" He burped mid-word. We laughed like little kids at this. He seemed almost excited at having been called "Doug".

"See? Perfect!" I yelled. "You burped saying 'Christ'."

"Right." He humoured me.

But I was relentless. He didn't have to know that my writing was itself conservative, that I too was a timid manipulator of form. Because now I was a gassy poet, a beery bombast.

And he didn't have to know how worried I was about my own work, and that I was ranting to myself.

"Break the rules," I yelled at him. "Run the red light." If I were a Buddhist priest I would have slapped him. "Go ninety. Kill someone. Smash the cop in the face. Ram the ambulance."

"You're absolutely right." He mocked me kindly.

"It fits!" I waved my arms around, indicating everything. "What doesn't fit? Tell me!"

The swimmer had left the pool, our bottles were empty. I searched the bar for evidence.

"Even we fit!" I hopped and wriggled my ass on the chair, to show him rebellion against form. "Both of us. Even someone as ugly as you!"

We got up and walked outside, toward the residence. Douglas had two more weeks here but tomorrow I was off for Vancouver. We'd be saying goodbye in the lobby. We walked slowly on the gravel path. I still wanted to help him out of his sadness—his music was confined, his life too much the other way.

It was a beautiful night, too precise a night to write down. It would end up merely words. A half moon lit the mountains, but didn't outshout the stars. All just so. I stopped.

"Look," I said.

We both looked up at the mountains and sky. Clichéed though it was—looking up at stars and wondering

on them—I couldn't help but see it all in light of tonight's
talk. Structure: here we were on manicured grounds,
ringed by buildings which were themselves contained by
mountains. An orbiting moon and path-bound stars, with
a lid of black over all of it.

I looked for the action. There: two ragged clouds
raced past, high, chaotic, their laws of forming and
unforming too small, too particular, for us to see.

And, closer: held by our own bodies, our breath
going in and out. Other than that, and the two clouds,
silence.

On the tip of my tongue was the poetic, bullshit
suggestion that he should draw measures across the night
sky—his studio had a skylight, he could do it with a magic
marker—and play the surprise opera denoted by the pat-
tern of the stars. But Douglas was already walking again,
cutting in through the trees. I caught up. When he tripped
on a bit of root I was going to pound it in yet again and say,
"Surprise!"

But then we heard the grunt.

One grunt, brief. The warning in it put my hair on
end. Neither Douglas nor I breathed now. There stood two
elk, not ten feet from us. The bull—with the antler rack, and
an erection that arced up the length of his belly—took a step
away. He limped. He'd been born crippled, or one foreleg
had broken and healed crookedly. The cow elk stood where
she was. Both bull and cow stared unblinking danger at us,
their four eyes reflecting the half moon. They looked
perfectly ready.

How long we stood waiting, not breathing, I don't
know. Douglas hooked a finger inside my elbow. We took
a slow step back. The elk watched this. A moment later,
they did the same. I realized I could smell them: old rugs,
grassy urine. We stepped back again. This second piece of

distance appeared to satisfy the bull. He turned from us, back to his mate. His erection, all of three feet, almost to the ground, had been shrinking. Now it lengthened and arced up fast, a powerful search.

Trees surrounded us all. The moon and stars cast shadows, repeating us all on the ground.

"Yes!" whispered Douglas as the bull mounted. His crooked foreleg gave him a weirdly certain grip on her back. The power of the first thrust sent them both tripping forward.

God, their breathing. I expect to hear it someday, in music.

THE WORK-IN-PROGRESS

Anthony Ott was in town tonight, said the poster. He would be reading from his latest work.

Theo studied the somewhat famous face. Stark black and white, the Xerox rendition shouted Ott's hollows and crags. His eyes were inscrutable blots. It was more a Rorschach than a face.

Theo caught himself memorizing the address. Why in heaven's hell would he want to hear Ott again? That time twenty years ago had been so horrible. He thought about it still. The spectacle. Ott singling him out, shouting, emphasizing the "you".

Since then, Theo hadn't bought any of Ott's books. In bookstores he found himself avoiding looking at their covers. Eight o'clock, Theo whispered, scanning the poster.

Also he hated readings on principle. He never went to one voluntarily. In the four years at this university he had been often forced by committee—risk to tenure was never mentioned, but there it was—to take on the chore of hosting yet another minor writer. A campus tour, dinner, then the reading itself, Theo sitting with ten or so self-conscious others in a sterile room of empty chairs, wishing he had a bottle of wine, a magazine or—this was deliciously perverse, given what he did for a living—a mini-TV so he could watch the ball game.

Even that first reading had been less than voluntary.

It had been a date, a first date, with Oona. A prof had mentioned a reading by some new writer named Ott and, later that night, there they were, driving to the suburban library, neither Theo nor Oona wanting to be the one to venture that this idea sounded a little dry. Both wanted nothing more than to find a bed somewhere, which they did eventually do, and did again and again for years until their sole reason for being together rubbed itself out.

Eight o'clock. A converted church. Theo stood before looming wooden doors, posters of Ott's face taped to them. He'd actually done it. He'd come, once more, to hear Anthony Ott read.

People filed by as he stood at the threshold. He had not yet committed himself. He would ponder this a moment. Why had he come? Was he bored? No. Did he want to relive memories of Oona? No. Youth? No. He was proudly pragmatic. He never loved what wasn't there.

So why? He felt a yawning in the gut. Ott had said, See *you* again.

Not that Ott could pull what he pulled last time, not with this many people—ten had pushed past him into the church in the last minute alone. The other time there had been just him, Oona and two old ladies. And Ott. In a windowless back room of the Valley library, Ott had loomed over them there in the front row. The only row. Maybe that had been part of Ott's problem, that so few had come to see him read.

Bearded, dark, he'd had an Abraham Lincoln severity, without height. His eyes were wise, but also mean. In a natural hierarchy logical to Theo at the time, Ott's wisdom gave him the right to be mean. He'd looked at the four of them in turn, then shaken his head and, well, sneered. At the scant number perhaps, or at what he'd seen, or not seen, in their eyes. It had made Theo nervous and, for some reason, ashamed.

Ott read from what he called a work-in-progress. It sounded like poetry. Odd syntax, obscure reference, and images that when given close attention granted a tweak in some dusk-lit landscape of the brain. Actually, Theo didn't listen much. Oona's bare knee was against his. Theo stared at it. He answered her pressure. She increased hers. He his. At one point, with Ott ten minutes into it, Theo's and Oona's legs were shaking in a push-of-war, and they were trying hard not to laugh.

Ott eventually finished, informed them that the book he had just read from was to be called *The Lobe*, then looked Theo in the eye and asked, loud, "Why did you come?"

"Me?" Theo asked. He couldn't tell if Ott had seen their game-playing, or if the question was simply interest.

"Why did you come?" Ott asked again. His expression wouldn't change.

"Ah, I wanted to hear you read. We"—best get Oona in on this, take some of the heat—"wanted to hear you read."

"I'm nobody. Do you go to every reading in town?"

"No." Theo almost added "sir".

"Tell me why you came. Tell me the truth."

Ott leaned onto his podium and he hung out over Theo, barely three feet away. Theo felt his face go red. He shrugged.

"I don't know." He turned to Oona and tried a joke. "Hey, why did we come here? I thought we were going to *Rocky II*."

"How long," Ott asked, "have you wanted to be a writer?"

"What?" Why torture just him? There were three others here.

"You want to be a writer, don't you."

"I dunno. Maybe. I've thought about it."

"So tell me a story."

"What?"

"You want to be a writer. Tell me a story."

"Right now?"

"I told you one. You tell me one. Be a writer."

Theo laughed weakly. He looked over at Oona, and she grimaced in sympathy.

Theo tried another. "I'll write one and mail it to you."

"Come on." Anthony Ott was severe. "Tell me a story."

"I can't just—"

"*Fucking tell me a story.*"

One old lady gasped. Theo glanced over. She gathered up her sweater, to leave. The other old lady was smiling.

Ott loomed over him, relentless. What the hell. A story. "Once upon a time, there was a boy and a girl with nothing to do. What they really wanted to do was go play doctor. Instead they went and heard a big man read a storybook." Theo wasn't saying this out loud, of course. "The big man read his storybook a long long time and put everyone to sleep. . . ." Some bizarre part of his brain was telling this to the main part that was shy and feverish and outraged. Here he was a minute away from sex with Oona in his parked car, and this monstrous bohemian was trying to humiliate him.

"When the story was over," Theo said to himself, watching Oona sort of smiling at Ott, "the man got very bossy and the boy began to cry."

"No story to tell?" asked Ott. He was smiling sarcastically, packing his briefcase.

". . . and he decided never, ever to buy that man's books."

Ott was leaving. Speak up now or forever hold. . . . At the door Ott turned and waved to the empty room, wearing a cheery smile. He pointed at Theo and yelled, "See *you* again."

Theo stood at the church doors, still undecided, when a nondescript fellow, the host, likely a lit drone clinging to tenure like himself, came out and said, "We're starting."

Theo looked for a seat. The place was packed. Sixty or so people had come to listen to Anthony Ott. A single empty seat in the front row, in front of the podium. All those seated in the row would be Ott fans. Would people think that of him too if he took that seat, even if it was the only seat?

Theo made his way to the glaring chair. He made a show of scanning back over the room, and shrugging before he sat down. And then he pointedly looked at his watch.

Suddenly Ott entered from the side. He strode to the podium, dishevelled, preoccupied, utterly not nervous, as though this reading were just another of the day's chores.

Theo stared up at the man. Twenty years. There was something obvious and repulsive about the bastard still.

Ott snapped open a battered briefcase. He lifted out a stack of paper which he thunked onto a shelf inside the podium. Age hadn't changed Anthony Ott much. A few pounds, some grey hair. Mostly, he looked twenty years wiser. And meaner.

"I'll read from a work-in-progress," he announced, looking down, shuffling the unseen stack. Theo hated it when he couldn't see the paper. He liked watching a pile dwindle, he liked being able to tell how much longer the ordeal would go on.

Ott looked up suddenly, as if remembering where he was. He began searching the eyes of the audience. He didn't hurry. Seat by seat, row by row, he met eyes. People began to shuffle. It was dreadful. Theo heard a snicker. Ott continued his scan. When he was almost through, almost up to Theo himself, Ott threw a match into the fumes of unease by saying, "I wonder why you're here."

The hall went into high fidget.

A vague dread had been growing in Theo's stomach ever since he first sat down. When their eyes did meet, Theo knew. He was sitting in the same spot exactly as on that horrid night past. Theo jolted upright with *déjà vu*. His spine rang. They stared at each other. It was like decades had passed in a night's sleep.

Then Ott's eyes moved on. But his lids had lifted in recognition, Theo was sure of it.

"Anyone with ideas for a title for this thing of mine," Ott announced, a sneer prying up his lip, "I'll gladly consider it." Some people laughed. "Not good at titles," he added. More laughs, though Ott had sounded serious.

Ott began to read. Theo did try to listen. Readings were torture.

It was like this: Ott described someone named Marty, a man who saw people as "scared carcasses fleeing a death so inevitable it had somehow already happened". Theo got caught pondering this notion and missed the next bit, about Marty reliving his mother's breast whenever he smelled a certain fabric. Or when he felt a certain fabric? Angry to have missed it, he missed some more. Now Ott was onto someone named Lulu. Lulu was a girlfriend, a woman obsessed with birds ever since she heard they'd evolved from dinosaurs.

"... her mind cradled the miracle," Ott read, looking up, "of a brontosaurus taking wing in the body of a tweeting finch. ..."

Theo was half-hearing all this. He was trying to recall

Ott titles, none of which he'd read. *The White Harpsichord*? *Call Me 26*? Weren't those two?

Theo sat up with a jerk. Ott was staring at him, saying, ". . . the worst part was that in public places Marty loved to point out any big step and say to her, 'Watch out. It's a lulu.'"

It was an accusing look. Though with Ott it was hard to tell what lay behind the eyes. But the bastard. The arrogance. What right had he to single out a daydreamer and stare at him? This wasn't school.

". . . her comeback with a louder 'Real funny Marty' always saw him instantly defeated, and recalculating the arithmetic of their love. . . ."

Had Ott indeed recognized him? He was back reading from the page now. Or was he just pretending to read? His lips moved, but not his eyes.

What had happened that night? Theo had left the library with an ugly, unfinished feeling. Motives shrouded, meanings hanging. He'd told Ott he wanted to be a writer. It was the only time he told anybody that. He hadn't even been sure of it himself until he heard himself say it out loud.

Theo had not become a writer. But neither was he jealous of writers, though Oona had accused him of this that night as he punched his bed between fits of lovemaking, cursing Ott. Oona assured him over and over that Ott hadn't made a fool of him, that Theo had stood his ground. Yet all through their relationship, whenever Theo tore into any writer, living or dead (it was his job as a student of literature, after all), Oona would say to him, simply, like it was truth, "You're jealous."

He'd given it a try. But it was almost as though he was too smart for creativity. It was like he knew too much in advance, his brain a tyrant that chided a mistake before it was even made. Theo saw this but could not stop it. Every good idea was analysed to woodenness before it was typed down and freed.

After several years of such trying, he quit. But he was not jealous. He'd admitted to himself without terror that the part of him that was able to "make stuff up" was hidden from him, or lost, perhaps in childhood. It was not a big deal. Intellect had overcome a certain instinct, a certain spontaneity. That was all. He was not jealous.

Eyes. Theo remembered where he was. Ott was staring again.

" . . . and the oily fur falling in handfuls from Marty's dog Mica drove Lulu nearly mad. . . ."

When Theo met his eye, Ott turned back to his pages. But it did indeed seem he was not reading at all. He was talking. Had he memorized this stuff? Was that possible?

" . . . it was birds she wanted. Birds. Birds! Flight. A pet at home in space. Not the mud bone blood tongue of dogs. . . ."

Theo checked his watch. Ott had been reading now for almost a half hour. A decent reading lasted forty minutes. An excellent reading lasted thirty.

Theo hoped Ott would at least be decent. He waited for voice intonations to rise to a final peaking sentence. He recalled one poet he'd hosted who had read on and on, almost an hour and a half. It was always lesser writers who read longest. Once they got hold of a stage they refused to let it go. Toward the end, over shuffling feet, the poet had read faster and faster, his face pale. Another thing about readings, Theo decided now, was that writers deserved whatever they got.

" . . . on his sixteenth birthday Marty received from his folks a truckload of dirt dumped in the back yard. He was told to level it and plant the vegetation of his choice. . . ."

So had Ott memorized this stuff? He was no longer reading. He stared at the ceiling, or over the heads of the audience. Or at Theo.

" . . . as far as the more exotic plants went, all he got was a single cantaloupe the size of a cat's head. . . ."

On and on and on. The reading approached the hour mark. The next time Ott eyed him, he would look pointedly at his watch.

" . . . it was Lulu's magic with flowers that seduced him. She could entice from dirt blooms the likes of which no one there had ever seen, blooms so huge with colour they shrieked, and were almost frightening. . . ."

On and on. Perhaps Theo slept. Because, when it came, the shout from several rows back had the effect of jolting him awake.

"Not this time, Ott!" a man yelled. A chair scudded on the floor.

Theo turned with everyone else to see a young fellow with wild hair stumbling out of his row. He wasn't looking at Ott. He made the aisle and stomped out of the church, mumbling.

Ott watched the retreating man. His voice rose as if following him out the door.

"Well. Suddenly, one day Marty just stopped growing things. He just gave up. Woe to him. Big mistake."

Ott looked down again to his pages, though Theo was certain now he wasn't reading.

" . . . his new hobby was no more than a distraction for his failure at flowers. . . ."

"You win!" someone yelled just behind Theo's head, making him jump. "That's enough! You win!"

Theo turned. A fat man behind him stood, red-faced, pointing at Ott. He held a suitcase. The airplane tags dangling from the handle looked fresh.

"I'm out of it!" the fat man yelled. He shoved his way out of his row and clomped puffing out of the church.

Ott read calmly on. A tiny smile lifted the corners of his mouth.

". . . distractions, one after another, blocking the light from a life. The travel, the TV and brownies and cookies and more of Auntie Em's chili and cornbread and, my goodness, Marty spun like a top in his search for the next wee thing to fill his skinny time. . . ."

Theo wondered if he should leave as well. He could hear others get up, some quietly, some with a grumble. He could hear whispers of grievance, of gathering mutiny. He thought he could hear one man softly weeping.

Theo didn't want to leave. He realized he was enjoying himself for the first time since it had started, over an hour ago. He looked at his watch. An hour and a half ago. That was enough, he joked to himself, to make any man cry.

He sat back in his chair. Perhaps Ott had a kind of cult following, people who travelled to all his readings, like fans of the Grateful Dead. Theo swivelled and checked out the audience. About a third had gone. The remainder looked to be of two types. One group seemed confused. They sat politely but wanted to leave. This strange author had gone on far too long, they seemed to be thinking. The other group was more resolute, angry, used to it. They looked dug in.

". . . there's a twist to this tale, that will without fail, save us from ruin, as sure as the mail. . . ."

God, the maniac was rhyming now. Theo listened. He heard iambic and dactylic, enjambment and inversion. Marty and Lulu kept popping in and out, as if to keep up the pretence of a story. But it all made a sort of sense, Theo thought, it seemed to be about something almost vital. Almost, well, personal. One's dirty underwear, or something. Theo could not put his finger on it. Whenever he thought he had, he realized he'd missed the next bit, the next clue, and his logic fell apart.

"... Marty went to bed. Marty slept all night long. Marty got up. Marty washed. Marty looked out the window. He said, Hello Mr. Sun. He had a good breakfast. Good Marty. Where was Lulu? Good Lulu. Lulu was not there. Lulu was not with Marty. . . ."

This was some kind of challenge, Theo decided. The church was now a quarter full. A dozen people. One man was snoring loudly, but it sounded fake, a provocation. Ott kept going, looking perfectly at ease. Twenty minutes later the snorer left.

" . . . Lulu sat in her kitchen too. Picture a split picture. He and her, staring at their phones. Lulu's phone is off the hook. She knows that Marty knows it's off the hook. And she knows that Marty knows that she knows that he knows. And she knows that Marty knows that she knows that Marty knows that she. . . ."

Theo looked up. He had decided. He no longer considered Ott a profoundly irritating human but rather a kind of natural force. An unclimbed mountain whose obstacles were boredom and spite. Ott walking in and opening his mouth had been a challenge from the start. An arrogant dare, a slap in the face with verbosity's gaudy white glove.

Theo would meet Ott's challenge. Whatever the game, Theo was going to win.

By midnight, four hours since the start, only Theo and one other man were left. Theo turned his seat around to study him. He was young, thirtyish, dressed in a blue track suit. He looked in shape. He looked prepared. He sat erect, eyes closed. He looked either asleep or in the bosom of some Eastern discipline.

Theo listened and didn't listen. Ott was now into Marty's childhood.

". . . with a pure innocence, Marty squished the frog. He was as innocent as the frog itself whenever it long-tongued a bug. Now it was frog's turn to be bug, Marty's to be frog. Sacred teeter and totter. Profane reason had not yet intruded on Marty. . . ."

Theo drifted in and out. Sometimes he sought day-dreams so as to escape Ott's words, some of which slipped in and squeezed him. He tried to recall Oona but couldn't, not her face. Parts of her body, yes. Which perhaps summed up their time together. He could recall the feeling of being inside her, as distinct from being inside other women. He could recall her voice too, he'd loved her voice. They'd had some good times. Lying in bed, no hurry, savage in their desire, no plan to life. How long you could sustain that kind of life was of course the whole—

"Marty oh Marty oh Marty!" Ott shrieked, imitating Lulu's voice. It sounded like Olive Oyl in "Popeye". "How could you how could you how could you . . . ?"

Theo thought of problems at work. Funding cuts for research. A tedious faculty in general, older types who talked Chaucer and Pope even in the lounge. Lately Theo had been admitting to himself that he didn't much like his work. To admit that about his life work was, well, horrible. But how many people truly liked their work? In their heart of hearts how many? The word itself was tiring. "Work" was synonymous with struggle. "Struggle" was onomato-poeia for "work". "Work" was anathema to "play". By definition work should not be liked.

One-thirty. Oooh, he'd be tired tomorrow. He had to prep a lecture. Virginia Woolf. Stream of . . . Jesus, he should just bring the class here, this loon would likely still be at it. Ott looked depressingly fresh.

"... No, I said, 'Lulu, will you MARRY me.' That's what I said. I didn't say, 'Lulu you scare me.' Why the hell would I say that? Because I do I do I do want to marry you...."

At a quarter to three Theo jolted upright at a crash behind him. The fellow in the track suit had toppled, chair and all. He lay on the floor and didn't move. Perhaps he was dead.

"I win!" Theo shouted, nearly delirious. He hadn't meant to.

"Please don't interrupt," Ott hissed at him, glaring briefly before turning back to his paper.

"... so Marty decided to read a book. What to read was always a problem because his library was so vast, taking up four walls in one room, and six walls in another...."

"Come on!" Theo yelled, out of anger and fear both. "What the hell! Let's go home!"

"Be quiet or I'll ask you to leave.... Books stacked on the toilet-back, up to the ceiling. Books filled the cellar, stacked on the cold floor. Last time he was down there he'd plucked an obscure Tolstoy from the mouse dust and shouted *Da*! like an overt Russian and curled up with it for two days and nights...."

Theo flopped back into his seat. He'd been sweating. It was the middle of the night. Rain pattered on the roof of the church. His dog would be whimpering in his spot under the eaves. His class tomorrow would be a disaster.

Theo stared at Ott. The writer was clinging to his lectern for support. He was holding his chin up, fighting gravity. He was definitely tiring.

"... the King of Persia had amnesia," Ott trilled in a raspy attempt at a little girl's voice. "... and tried to rob the store. Apackalips, apocalypse, he went back again for more...."

The lunatic was rhyming again. Theo stood up. He waggled a finger, groping for words.

"You just made that up. It doesn't count."

Ott stopped and looked up at Theo. His brows rose in supercilious innocence.

"This is my novel-in-progress. Please don't interrupt."

"A novel? You're saying this is a novel? Okay, where does that Persia thing fit in? And what does it mean?"

"It was Lulu's rhyme. She is a child and she's skipping. You think a child's rhyme must..." Ott pronounced the next word as if it crawled with maggots "...'mean'? You an English professor?"

Theo said nothing.

"Be quiet or I will be forced to stop." Ott paused like a shark before the fatal bite. "Would you...like me to stop?"

Two very distinct sides of Theo's mind had a quick, shocking fight, and the perverse side won.

"Of course not." Theo had his own sense of timing. "I came all this way."

He watched Ott for a sign of disappointment or fear, but saw nothing. Ott merely continued. He wore the tiniest smile.

"Lulu wound her skip-rope in a tight figure eight and went in for lunch. For the past ten minutes her nostrils had been ripe with the anticipation of her daily Velveeta...."

Oh, but Theo was hungry. Ott must be too. Expending all that energy. Look at him, still bobbing his head for emphasis, still gazing out at a crowd that wasn't there. The rain had stopped. His voice rang louder in the silence.

Oh, my. Crazy, crazy. Ott, Ott, wouldn't stop, wouldn't stop and wouldn't drop, talking till his head went pop. There, put that in your "novel". I can do drivel too, Mr. Writer. Why am I listening to you, not you to me? Old old

Anthony Ott, drops his trousers on the spot. Behind the dais lurks a penis. Against the podium he bumps his scrotium.

Why the hell had he given up on writing, anyway? Maybe he should try again, quit the analytical maze. Right, quit his job at his age. He was thinking crazy. Oh, it was late.

"Would you like to go for a coffee?"

Ott had spoken to him. He had stopped reading and asked a question. He had distinctly said, Would you like to go for a coffee. Theo sprang to his feet and punched his fist in the air.

"Yes! Coffee!" he shouted. "I win! Me! I win!"

Theo stood teetering. He grinned, puffing. Ott was watching him. A smile rose like sewer water.

"Please shut up," Ott said calmly, smile peaking in a sneer. "Don't interrupt. MARTIN has just asked LULU if she cared to join him for coffee. It's pivotal."

Theo was breathing through his mouth. He stared past Ott into the velvet-curtained gloom of the empty stage. Ott cleared his throat and continued.

" . . . 'Java preference where we go?' Martin asked of his love. 'It shouldn't mocha lot of difference. . . .'"

Theo quietly took his chair. It was getting light out. The door opened and he turned to see a janitor enter, take a fearful look at them and begin sweeping. Ott's voice gained volume.

" . . . Marty suggested that in their role as the custodians of truth, the lumpen should never jumpen to conclusions. . . ."

Theo couldn't quit, he couldn't let the bastard win. Ott looked too content, in a bliss of his own making. Somehow he knew he had in his grip a professor of literature.

During Ott's pauses, Theo could hear birds out on the eaves. Beaky rhymes and gibberish. Nature, mocking him too.

Such noise. Where in hell was he. Theo opened his eyes to darkness. He could hardly breathe. His spine arched in pain.

Awareness limped in. Theo discovered that his face lay on his knees, his nose pinched between them. His arms hung down, knuckles scraping the gritty linoleum. The noise was a dreadful monotone voice. Theo remembered where he was.

" . . . Phenomenology is a body of heavily thought thought aimed at that which exists beyond thought. While we work hard thinking, Phenomeness dances with her cruel girly grin, singing Nya nya nya nya nyaa nya. We can hear this tune, some nights, issuing from the stars. . . ."

Anger fueled a burst of adrenalin. Trailing a wire of saliva, Theo's head lifted off his knees.

"Bullshit!" Theo croaked. "You're babbling!"

". . . that's what Phenomeness sings, SAID LULU, AS MARTY WOKE FROM HIS NAP."

"That's a trick. Doesn't count. You're just making it up."

Ott sneered joyously. "Tolstoy 'just made up' *War and Peace*, you insignificant bugger. Go back to sleep and don't interrupt me or," the pause, "I'll have to ask you to leave."

Theo let his head fall. He rolled his eyes under his lids in an attempt to relubricate them. Behind him, a crash. He turned to see the janitor stack the last chair, save Theo's. He rammed it onto the top of the stack with unnecessary force, glaring at Ott all the while. Then he began sweeping the cleared space, over-clomping his work boots.

" . . . so what the hell and what the heck, they swept the house and then went camping, a final attempt to love nature before either it was gone or they were. Lulu was the one who figured out both the tent and the camp stove.

Marty angrily stacked firewood. Next morning, they woke in sleeping bag grunge and shrieking clouds of mosquitoes, surrounded by the snoring, still-drunk bodies of local hot-car teens, who used the provincial park to party. Perhaps, Marty hoped, they were nature lovers too. . . ."

Theo relaxed his muscles and tried not to think about food. He hand-helped himself up and stiff-legged it to the bathroom for a fierce morning pee. The temptation to just carry on into the sunny street was almost impossible to resist. Food. Sleep. Life. His class was beginning in twenty minutes.

But so what. There would be other classes. Other jobs even. You could only beat Ott once.

He returned. He continued to listen and not listen. The janitor shouted something in a foreign language and left, trying but failing to slam the heavy church door. Around noon a gaggle of old people poked their heads in, perhaps to convene a meeting. Ott's now-robotic delivery and lone scowling disciple made short work of them.

Theo had become aware of an interesting part of his mind. It was as if a part of him would let go, into delirium or sleep, simply not caring what happened. At that point his thoughts would take off. Roiling, jumping, goofy but strangely wise. Story lines and rants and scenic descriptions. The oddest part was that for entire minutes he'd be unclear exactly whose voice he was hearing, his own or Ott's.

". . . he tried and tried to find the bird beautiful. To love it. Marty decided that unless he loved it in the next ten minutes, he was going to build a slingshot and kill it. . . ."

Theo found himself not so much criticizing Ott's story as adding to it, making it his own. I can do this too, Theo told himself. I can make stuff up too. And, ha ha, I don't even care.

Theo looked quickly up at Ott. That was it. Ott was working hard to stand up, certainly, but he wasn't working at telling his story. He was just telling. And he didn't care.

That was it. Not care. Not work. Just let it go and tell whatever came, just tell, now, as it arrived, now, as it came in its fresh and bright—

"Would you like to have some breakfast with me?"

Theo went stiff. Very slowly, he lifted his eyes to Ott. Ott was staring at him. Smiling kindly.

"Would you care to get breakfast at some café?"

Theo closed his eyes and smiled at the world. He stretched his arms wonderfully, glory bursting in every joint.

"Okay," he said. "Sure. It's been quite a long—"

"YES I WOULD LIKE BREAKFAST, SAID LULU. ANYTHING BUT THESE BEANS AND SHIT WITH SAND IN IT."

Ott's eyes bugged out, full of contempt. He smiled like a panting dog. He enunciated carefully, as if to a child, "If you don't stop interrupting, I'll have to—"

Theo launched himself. He went for Ott's face, but Ott was surprisingly quick, manoeuvring the podium as a shield against Theo's slaps. Ott looked surprised, but pleased.

Theo could hear himself actually growling. He might have broken a knuckle on the podium. He didn't care. He wanted Ott. Dragging the podium, backstepping, the bastard still wouldn't stop talking.

"... by now it was clear Marty didn't like nature. The tides, the dirt, a cold blast of wind on his city-ass face. Poor schmuck couldn't take it. ..."

Theo tried kicks at Ott's feet. He smashed his ankle on the podium base.

"... soon he'd flee back to civilization and sterility.

Nature would continue without him. . . ."

"Shut up!" Theo screamed, hopping, still advancing, holding his ankle. "Shut up!"

" . . . without him, without him, without him. Lulu, standing in the wind outside her tent, wouldn't even remember his name. . . ."

"Shut up! Fake!"

" . . . Ah, memories of Lulu, memories of the carnal tent, no-holds-barred sweetness and spit. . . ."

"Cheat!" Theo shouted, hoarse. "Chimp!"

" . . . the sex of rain on the face, the lust of raw food to the famished. . . ."

"I know what you're doing!"

Theo suddenly stopped pursuing. Standing, breathing hard, he gave an exaggerated shrug, his palms ending up level with his ears. "It's no big deal, Ott."

Anthony Ott paused where he was. He set the podium upright and leaned on it.

"Marty faces the wind and has an idea," Ott said quietly. He looked intently at Theo, one eyebrow raised.

"Marty's not me," Theo said, approaching, not knowing what he was going to say until he said it. "And Lulu does whatever you tell her to."

"Nope. Too bad. Seems Marty's still trying to think his way out of it." Ott stood his ground as Theo came closer. "Maybe some day he'll be brave enough to tell a story."

"Oh bullshit, Ott," Theo said through his nose and teeth. They were now face to face, foreheads an inch apart. "I've been telling myself a story all my life. . . ."

"Marty's been masturbating in the china cabinet?"

"I'm not damned arrogant, like you. I don't spew it at everyone. You have no shame."

Nose to nose, Theo could see the wild crimson veins on Ott's eyeballs. His eyes were beady and savage, amoral.

There was sleep goo in the corners. Theo saw dirty pores, and single hairs coming crazy out of his cheeks. He could smell his breath, coffee and meat and stale liquor.

Looking into Ott's eyes, Theo suffered a strange shift in perception. For a second, he thought he was looking at himself. For a second, Ott was him. He Ott. It felt wild and frightening, a cold wind blasting out of nowhere.

"Shame is constipation, said Lulu. And embarrassment is a sin." Ott tilted back his head in a pose of grand arrogance. Theo could see up his nostrils.

"Lulu's egomania," Theo found himself saying, "is boring."

Ott brightened. "Shyness turns smart people into dweebs." He leaned forward, pressing his forehead against Theo's. He hissed. "DWEEB."

Theo grabbed Ott's neck and squeezed. "Lulu's gonna die, SAID MARTY."

"Dweeb," Ott croaked. "Thinker. Pick-apart."

They fell to the floor and rolled, Theo still choking Ott.

"Marty squeezed harder," Theo said through his teeth, "and Lulu turned red. The smile fell off her like the leprous wings of a...."

"Yeah. Tell me a story, Dweeb...."

"...rotting flying dinosaur!"

"Fancy pants...." Ott could hardly speak.

"Animal."

"Anal...brain...." Ott's voice trailed off into silence and his eyes closed.

"Pig," whispered Theo. "Child"

Ott said nothing this time. Theo thought he might be dead.

Suddenly Ott rolled to the side, out of Theo's hands. "Nya nya nya nya nyaa nya!"

Ott leapt up and Theo chased him. Gasping, their arms hanging sloppily, they ran around the empty church, Theo following Ott's zigzags. Ott tittered like a young girl. Once he stopped, spun to face Theo and roared like a monster. Theo hesitated a second, and Ott ran away again laughing.

When Ott tried to climb the stage, Theo got a hold of a leg. He pulled Ott, shrieking, to the floor. Again they wrestled, Theo ending up on top.

"It's never gonna stop!" Theo screamed.

"You're right!" Ott screamed back. And then stopped struggling. Both of them gasped for breath. Theo sensed that something was over. Looking into Ott's eyes, which were passive now, he again felt the awful shift, that Ott's eyes were his own.

Ott smiled, and nodded once. For some reason Theo got off. Ott climbed to his feet slowly, helping himself with his hands. He limped to Theo's chair, which had been knocked over. He set it on its legs facing the stage and, groaning, sat down.

"It's your turn," Ott said quietly, shifting in the chair to get comfortable. "Tell me a little story."

THREE INCREDIBLE STORIES ABOUT EAGLES

Absent of shapely lies to tell, I've decided to try truth for a change. Because I have a good true story. But I see immediately that truth has a huge flaw. It puts me in the cheap comedic position of saying, No, this is real, I swear. And you will believe me or you won't.

Just as cheap is a writer writing about writing. But I have to. If I began as a normal story, with none of this talk, and you assumed it to be fiction, the story would lose its power. Truth rarely has the shape, the totality, that fiction—art—demands. Here: the sinking of the *Titanic* would have been but a tragic and gaudy adventure story. One pictures Shelly Winters, Ernest Borgnine *et al.*, floundering about. But it being true—this biggest, safest ship ever, sinking in a wash of jewels and hubris on her first voyage—makes it magnificent. Or Carlos Castaneda: if his stories are true they are incredibly good.

Not that my three stories are titanic, or wise. The point is, their power comes from their being true.

It was the sitting here now, storyless, that reminded me of the first eagle. On that day too, years ago, I recall being unable to conjure up anything to write about. Waiting at the window, not even looking. Then, like a cartoon lightning bolt, there it was.

I was renting a one-room cabin up the coast, so homely and isolated it was gift-cheap. It perched on a rock just ten feet from the high-tide line of a deep bay. From the window I could almost spit on the resident mergansers paddling in the seaweed. Woody Woodpecker top-notches quivering, mergansers are wall-eyed, jerky, stupid even for birds. They aren't eagles.

I was staring out the window, I suppose waiting for inspiration, for a new twist on things. Living alone in a cabin with no phone or TV, and nothing to do but make meals, write letters to Molly, go for walks, I was drowning in the ordinary. Weather. Creaky floor. My own breathing. A sigh would make me self-conscious. The shock was all the more violent because as I stared out the window I was in a sort of trance, not at all a wise one, just a hum of small-thought, like near-sleep.

This first eagle story actually begins with a seal. There I was at the window, staring. The water was glassy—a mirror, perhaps. Then, bang, right in front of me, black and leaping. The twenty-foot distance felt like an inch. Exploding the glass surface, the seal shot two-thirds of its body-length out. In its teeth was a ling cod, a wild skinny one, two feet long. The seal broke water already shaking its head like a dog with a rag, whipping and snapping the cod-body, instinct's spasm to break the main bones and make this thing dead. Spray came off in a rainbow arc.

It would have been gorgeous even had I expected it, gorgeous even on TV, a reel of nature's greatest hits. Blasting my waking sleep as it did, its effect was lethal. I was car-accident awake. But it wasn't over. Here is the incredible part, the part least likely to be believed. The seal had been whipping the rag-doll cod for just two or three seconds. I don't know if the seal let go by accident, but its next whip tossed the cod up a few feet into the air. It hung there in a slow twisting roll when *smut* (I could hear it through the window), an eagle on a line out of nowhere suddenly had the cod by the head and was bearing it away, floppy and long from its talons. The huge bird's regal flapping, not slowed by its impact with the cod, had it out of sight in seconds. I recall hugely powerful shoulders. The seal ducked and disappeared, perhaps in fear of a sudden god.

Well, so. It's not like ling cod or seal or bald eagles were rare around there. I doubt a week passed when I didn't pick out an eagle's white head at the top of a fir, or see one hanging up in the wind. I caught and ate ling cod. Seals slid off rocks when I rowed near; several times a seal had stolen a salmon that had tired on my line, near the boat. None of this makes a story.

What makes a story is that perfect pass, that impossible acrobats' timing. Leap-thrash-toss-*smut*! What makes the story is that coming-together-at-once, a savage clockwork so improbable it seemed sacred. As I told Molly at the pay phone later, the whole bit was over in five seconds, and I almost didn't believe it myself.

It remains a tight little memory, an anecdote to use now and then, a colour-maker at a party. Though I don't think people quite believe it. And yet of the three stories this first is the easiest to believe.

I think it was during that same phone call to Molly, when I described the seal-cod-eagle, that we planned our Long Beach rendezvous. So there was a connection between story one and story two, however slight.

* * *

Molly may read this. I want to tell it well. I want to witch her back into the mood of it, I want her to feel it in her gut. I want this because, though she was there, she may have been tempted in the meantime to doubt it ever happened.

But I also want Molly to examine her losses since

then, and decide. The underlying truth, unbelievable as it may be, is hers to discern. I've heard her hair has gone grey, too fast. I've heard about some colourful problems with relationships, and I've heard that she's stopped writing completely.

Molly and I would link up every month or so. This went on for years, so whatever it was we had, persisted. Our linking up would be fiery the first night, then we'd settle to an easy housekeeping mode, a nesting. We'd be great friends, lots of laughter. After a few days of this it was as if we woke up to the fact that it was so easy, so right. "Easy to do this forever" hung unspoken in the air. We'd suddenly fall afraid, and Molly especially would get moody, fighting about nothing for no reason. She'd eventually hint at her fear of "ending up" somewhere with somebody. Though I hear this is what she has done.

She was a writer too—a poet, and so perhaps more concerned with truth than me. She was a brooder, given to silence. Her main desire was to see behind things: to read a fern's luminescence, to let a whiff of mushroom shift her mood, to actually see the wind eating at the rocks.

At Long Beach we walked in spring cold along a vast quarter-moon of sand. We'd chosen the emptiest beach. Humans, including us, Molly said, easily stole power from this place. She believed that these misty Pacific reaches withdrew their best secrets when "clomped on by tourists", as she put it. Her movements economical, she walked the beach in quiet respect. Respecting that, I did the same.

We hadn't seen each other for three months and the nature of our intimacy was once again up in the air. We couldn't quite talk about it. I recall a stilted chat about contraception which got left hanging. We sipped B&B from her flask. When we did talk it was of these things: the psychological effects of living near such an eternal roar of surf; that new A-frame gouged into the beachfront woods; the likelihood that if we drank enough it would make a swim possible.

We almost stepped on the eagle. It was almost into rot, and its eyes had been eaten.

Molly stopped, rigid. It was as if she had stumbled onto a bag of forbidden money.

"I have to take a talon," she said.

We hovered over the bird. Its tiny white head-feathers were delineated by dirt. Molly's plight, evident in her voice, was that of a loving archeologist's. On her ledges and tabletops at home were bones, feathers, little skulls. A sketch of an eagle hung over her bed.

So here was treasure. But do you take King Arthur's bones home with you? In Pompeii do you dislodge the stone baby from the stone mother curled over it? Such was this beach's cradling: the soft wind, surf-moan, the eagle half held by the sand.

Molly went red in the face. Something got the better of her. (Do you think so now, Molly?) She crouched and began to tug a claw. Then she smacked the foot with a rock. I handed her a broken mussel shell, and it cut through the foot-leather at a knuckle. The tendons underneath were much tougher, like a strange metal. Molly sawed and sawed. Tired of waiting, I found another shell and selected a talon for myself.

When I began to cut, an eagle trilled.

An eagle's treble voice suggests a bird a quarter of its size. It's at once melancholy and shrill. We turned and saw the bird, sitting in a wind-weirded pine, fifty feet away at the treeline. We stared at it. It trilled again.

This was its mate we were hacking at. It was so obvious we didn't even have to voice it. The eagle had.

"Jesus," I said.

Whatever it was overcame Molly again. When she turned from the eagle in the tree, hissed, "I'm sorry," and stooped back to her talon, her face showed a mind torn cleanly in two.

The bird trilled again.

"Jesus," I said. I bent back to work as well. "Hurry. We're torturing the poor thing."

Molly felt so bad she couldn't speak. She hacked and hacked. The living eagle trilled every twenty seconds or so. When we stood up with our severed prizes, it flew off.

Our walk back toward the car was a guilty one. We each had a long black talon in a pocket. We talked about our guilt, about the sanctity of things, said what the hell, tried to laugh. We reminded ourselves that native Indians collected such things in abundance, and cherished them. We would cherish our talons.

We'd not covered much of the two-mile walk when we heard another trill. There was the eagle, perched on a snag at the treeline. We had no doubt it was the same eagle. It sounded the same, looked the same, chose the same distance from which to confront us. It watched us with the same eyes, eyes much better than ours, eyes that had no doubt seen every detail of us putting pieces of its mate in our pockets and walking them away.

"Great," I said.

Molly began to walk faster.

Do you remember all of this, Molly? Didn't it happen exactly this way? I know I'm making you out to be a bit more the villain, but this is how I saw it.

The bird flew off and reappeared and cried from another tree every few minutes. We could do little but talk about the eagle. Maybe eagles mated for life, I suggested. That seemed to be the case, Molly agreed, darkly. Maybe, I said, eagles have no concept of death, and the damn thing has been waiting and waiting for its mate to get up off the sand. That's probably it, Molly whispered. And now we, she added, have crippled it so it can't get up. Its mate blames us. Oh Christ, I said as the eagle called again, it's a fucking bird. It can't think. It's running on instinct. Are we supposed to go back with some crazy glue or something? We didn't kill it. At least now that eagle—I pointed to it trilling its head off as we passed in front of it—has a scapegoat.

Molly pretended to feel better.

The bird flew off at my pointing, trilling again. It sounded almost cheery by now, we were so used to it. I recalled hearing that songbirds in Latin America were caught and sold in markets after having acid droppered in their eyes. It blinded them and they were in agony, but they had no facial expression and were unable to produce a sound other than their famous song. They sang nonstop as mom and dad tourist smiled at the pretty birdies and reached for their money.

We were almost back at the start of the beach and could see Molly's car in the distance. Near the car, between it and us, was a black speck, something on the sand. I noticed it because it didn't belong. It looked movable in the wind, fragile.

I think I knew right away, though it took another hundred feet, and certainty, to stand my hair on end. I'd never, ever, seen an eagle standing on the ground, let alone in a parking lot.

Though they can fly thousands of miles and find a particular tree in a mess of forest, birds aren't very smart in the conventional sense. We don't usually think of them making connections like: Those humans are heading for that car way over there, so I'll just go wait for them by it. But that is what this eagle was doing. I've since thought of an explanation: with those eyes, that eagle had no doubt seen countless humans climb in and out of countless cars, so why wouldn't it make the connection, a fairly simple one of movement and shape and colour?

Still, an eagle waiting for us at the car, blocking our way, sounds horror-movie cheap, I know. Though believable enough. And it doesn't get any worse in that way, no devil-bird going for our eyes, nothing Hollywood at all. The severed talons didn't twitch or start to stab at us in our pockets. No, the eagle stood its ground until we were maybe forty feet away. It trilled at us as it took off, shitting a string of white as it did, but I've seen that as they fly from trees. Then it flew away without looking back.

Though I have no idea how far it may have followed the car.

What do you think, Molly? I haven't seen you since that weekend, where we struggled in sexual fever and then puzzlement about the nature of an "us", frightened by it. Then we went our separate ways, with eagle talons. I remember us admitting to each other at one point: most married couples loved less than us. After saying this, we were shy of each other, and you seemed almost angry.

In the weeks that followed it was the talons that came between us, and kept us apart from that time on. So, Molly, you're in this next story too.

* * *

The third story is the simplest to tell, though its meaning—what truth is behind it—is the hardest to figure.

I returned to my cabin on the bay and tried to write. What I tried to write, I have no idea. But fiction of some sort. I remember being unable to think up anything remotely remarkable, anything at all seductive. I must have been very blocked, because that same afternoon, not hesitating even a day, I hiked up to the knoll. The Compass.

Because it was over an hour's walk, I used the knoll only every few months, for special occasions: crises in my life or work, maybe a solstice if I remembered it, that sort of thing. I called it The Compass because of the four pines which surrounded it and, to my eyes at least, marked the four directions.

It was a striking place, really. After a long scramble through salal and forest you came to a mossy wall of granite, climbed it and found yourself on a bald rock dome overlooking the Strait, surrounded by nothing but these four big pines. Because the trees grew at the knoll's base, when you were on the knoll their tops were at the level of your head.

The view was stunning. I was instantly calmed by it. It made me understand the cliché "breath-taking". In any case, it forced me to relax, to just sit there, my gaze settled on vastness. In the face of such a sight my thoughts would automatically ease off, as if they sensed they amounted to nothing much here.

I took the knoll personally. I suppose this is why the third encounter with eagles affected me as it did. Since it happened there, how could I not help but take the eagles personally too?

I climbed the granite and stepped up onto the knoll. It was a clear afternoon, hot. The air shimmered, and smelled like sauna. I looked up into the sky, then out over the water. I had the talon in my pocket. My thoughts still tumbled and scurried, not yet overcome by the calm. Maybe I thought about fiction. Maybe, Molly, I was thinking about you. Maybe all thoughts are the same, at their root.

The first eagle was bad enough. There it was, staring at me from the west tree, just fifteen feet away, and at the level of my head. The back of my neck froze, hair lifted.

Eagles are timid birds despite their size: it should have flown at the sight of me.

I was actually backing up, afraid, when from over my shoulder I saw another eagle staring at me from the south tree.

I said to myself, eagles are not social birds. I grew more afraid. My stomach dropped away when I thought to look at the north tree. I made a low, animal noise when I saw the third one. And when I swung around to the east, to the tree I'd walked not five feet past to get onto the knoll, I knew I'd see the fourth eagle as well.

So. Four eagles, surrounding me on the knoll, head high. Looking at me. I was very aware of the talon in my pocket. Birds don't have facial expressions, and they showed nothing while I backed away in terror.

And that's it. What more can I say? Should I pretend to know if it meant something?

Any interpretation I put on these events has no more bearing than anyone else's interpretation. I would not for a second want to suggest that animals are psychic, or magical-mystical-wise or whatever. Another reason I've not told these stories is because I get embarrassed that anyone might think I could believe such impossibilities. But all I know is, it was impossible for those eagles to be there, gathered around me, unafraid, one day after I took a talon from Long Beach.

Yet that's what happened. Again I'm put into the position of having to say: It's true, I swear it. And it wasn't as if they did anything unreal. They didn't suddenly dip forward with their beaks and stab out their own entrails. They didn't suddenly become magical beings—it wasn't Carlos Castaneda. They didn't teach me a damn thing. I've since tried to find a meaning, and sometimes I think I almost have it. But I don't want to add anything false, I don't want to build onto truth, or twist it. I think it's a story worth telling without that.

And maybe it isn't finished. Maybe there are four stories. And maybe the fourth one isn't over yet:

I ran as far as I could, always looking back up into trees. Though I could see no eagles I had no doubt I was being seen. I reached my cabin. I considered hiking farther, to the gas station, to phone Molly and warn her and urge her to pick me up and take us back to Long Beach. But instead, I surrendered the talon myself, there in front of my cabin where I saw that first eagle. It felt superstitious as hell, but I was that nervous. I wanted to do it right away.

Standing at water's edge, easing it out of my pocket, I saw that the knobby knuckle had worked loose at the top of the talon. I pulled it and, trailing the knuckle bone, like lobster meat out of the claw-thumb, was shocking, talon-shaped meat of brightest red, almost day-glo. It looked alive, though that is superstitious as can be.

Holding the hollow talon in one palm and its inner meat in the other, I looked up for an eagle. I knew I wouldn't see one. I didn't know the equation, but surprise had something to do with this whole affair. Apologizing to the dead eagle, I tossed its pieces into the water, watched them sink away into the green depths and then walked to the store to phone you, Molly.

Do you remember that call? You didn't believe what I was saying even as I was saying it. I remember the feeling in my gut when I asked you where your talon was, and you said it was at the jewellers being mounted on a silver chain.

It was funny you didn't believe me. You were always the moony, superstitious one, believing in tides and spells and the witchiest of things. Or maybe you did believe me.

I remember now that, as I warned you, your silence had the tone of someone welcoming any power the talon might hold, even a power that went a wrong way.

You were angry when we hung up. We haven't talked since, and you haven't answered the letters.

You'll be reading this someday if it finds its way into some book or magazine. Though I haven't used your real name, a friend of yours will read it and because of the talon at your neck he will be reminded of you and give it to you and you'll read it and your neck will freeze and you will finally believe the third story. Maybe I'm being superstitious to suggest that your life's bad luck—your grey hair, your failures at poetry and at love—has anything to do with this. But think of the years that have passed and what has happened to you in them.

Or has not happened. You feel this loneliness, and the dark. You'll know deep in your gut that you should never deny something you know to be true.

Maybe it's not too late for us.

Molly, you can feel I haven't made anything up.

Only you can know the truth of this. Only the lucky or the cursed know the truth of luck or curses.

THE SUMMING OF THE PARTS

SETTINGS. Tonight Jack found himself—that is, happened on a moment of clarity—while pissing in a urinal. It was a bar he and friends had frequented when young. Bored, staring at the wall, a little drunk, pissing, eyes absorbed in the beige tile with its changeless crude rhymes, he saw something about time, how he'd flown over a span of it. Something said to him: Remember. And he remembered now so clearly how he'd often stood right here, in front of this same porcelain mouth, peeing. He'd been excited then, bouncing as he peed, excited with the fact of beers under his belt, the parties later, the women unknown, excited with the stronger juice of youth. But here he was years later. Nothing had changed but him. A boy beside him bounced, humming—at times gasping—a song Jack didn't know. Jack felt dull. Used. A question came out of nowhere: used by what?

Standing on a rock at low tide. The rock is maybe a quarter-acre large, made round by ebb and flow. There's a depression in its middle where the tide water stays behind, a small lake, and I looked down at the sea urchins purple and yellow, and mauve starfish, and some of the spiny kind. If I lift a rock, tiny eels panic at their home gone. It is windless, and there's my face in the water. My ordinary face made splendid—such is the work of a natural mirror. The overview it grants stays with me as I turn back to my probing of rocks and creatures. I watch myself as if from above, playing like a child.

At the Atlantic News, the literary journal rack stands across from the skin mag section. Leafing through a *Paris Review*, Behn stood ass to ass with a small man trying to make himself smaller, huddling over a glossy display of breasts. When the timid voyeur saw Behn watching him he slapped the magazine shut, shoved it back, hunched into his collar and fled. Another porn-gazer saw this but didn't move. Unique in his defiance, he stood mid-aisle, legs apart, arms held out boldly, naked pages splayed wide, not caring who saw—no, caring that everyone saw—that he was looking at male bodies, penises erect and oiled. The man was broad-shouldered, and wore a pony-tail. Behn assumed him gay.

It came on her for no discernible reason, but at this moment Dr. Smol's head felt like a big balloon. No, more: a zeppelin, huge. At the same time it felt small as a grain of salt. Infinite and infinitesimal both. What was worse, the grain of salt contained the zeppelin. A universe, driven to a density untenable. She'd had this before, maybe as a child, for she remembered it. Now, though, she was at the lectern of a large hall, speaking to the Convention of Physicians against Nuclear Proliferation. She had just introduced herself, and was halfway through her first sentence. Stunned by the condensed eternity her head had become, the second half of the sentence, said very slowly, was "... and though we are all doctors, we will die as quickly as everyone ... and then, like everyone, we will know."

PLOTS. Leaving the bar, Jack took the wheel, then looked across at his wife, who was angry at being dragged out like that, no reason given. He hadn't looked at her so closely, he realized, for years. He saw the big pores of her nose, remembered he'd considered them before marrying her. But over the years they, like all else, had joined the weave of a most forgettable fabric. She saw his face and said, What is it? He didn't answer her, but his mind answered itself, saying You Me Car Kids Life Piss Fuck Death Time Why. They got home, paid the sitter, and Jack's wife spun away from him in an insulted snit. Toward the bedroom. Oh, he dreaded following, lying beside her in silence. He'd sleep, and have the bad dream again. So there in the hall he grabbed her arm, knowing even as he did so that he wanted a mother. She slapped him, for the first time ever. So she was feeling it too, in her case a violence condensed by years. He left in a cab. It was eleven. He had to work tomorrow, but he didn't care. He told the cabby to drive him to the airport. He supposed he was drunk. He thought of his baby son Tucker, and what kind of life he would have. Jack had a credit card, and names of distant cities came to him unbidden.

The tide swells in quick and worries me off the rock, and I wade three feet of swirl to get back onto sand. I still feel young. The day is glorious as days can get. Perhaps my play has touched it. And as if to answer my mood, or tease it, there she is. As naked as me, but more used to it, a denizen of this wide-open place. Her walk is noble, unafraid. One can tell she prefers solitude, but doesn't mind me seeing her. Her tiny glasses add to her nudity. She carries a book, which makes her seem wise. Her name is May, I will learn, and wise she is, though as it turns out not in ways I've encountered before. I say hi in the most noncommittal way I can, which of course commits me completely. Her hi is so friendly, so rich, I know that if sex is to be a part of this we'll have to take several steps back into something more primitive. I stand aimlessly. She sees my inability to act, and then does something I'll all my life be thankful for. She raises the book, points to the title, which is too distant for me to read. Then she beckons me with a finger.

And wouldn't you know he followed Behn out of the Atlantic News? Perhaps Behn had glanced over at him and his books of naked men once too often. Behn knew he was feeling much as a woman must feel: perhaps pursued, but not threatened enough yet to say anything. Finally the man did catch up. He did position himself so as to speak. Behn tensed, afraid now and feeling ridiculous for it. The worst result would be a quaking awkwardness. Side by side they walked for half a block. Now he was afraid truly. Shoulder to shoulder with a bigger man, gay, silent, hunting. Behn recalled the fistfights he'd had playing hockey, how poorly he'd done, slapping wildly like a girl. Behn's stomach dropped out when the man started to laugh. A squeaky laugh, high in the throat, not a right laugh for this size of man. Then the man spoke. "Remember me?"

Dr. Helen Smol continued talking. Her address took a turn unforeseen to her as she abandoned her notes—data concerning the disruption of medical care in immediately post-nuclear rural regions—and began to speak from her widening mind. Her second sentence was, "And at collective death we will all know all reasons, and we will know only then if we should have tried harder, or if this was our necessary fate." Having no prop of papers at which to stare, she scanned the audience, an audience of hundreds surprised, unsettled, shifting in their seats. Her eyes settled on a man in the front row. He was unshaven, his clothes rumpled, his eyes red. He looked hung over, though it was night. He stared up at her with great intention. It came to Helen Smol that this man and she were of like minds. More, that he was encouraging the direction of her speech. As she recognized this, he smiled, the saddest smile Dr. Smol had ever seen. And then he nodded to her, an act that served to join them for good, and to bless her mind and nudge it off on its expanding journey, past the point of returning.

COMPLICATIONS. Jack had taken a flight to Vancouver. When it stopped in Calgary, he got off. He'd never been to Calgary. He wandered. Ten o'clock, a Saturday night, the place looked festive enough. More booze? His head pounded, but no. He'd find a hotel, he'd sit on the bed, he'd sit and consider. Something gigantic needed thought. No, it was beyond thought—something irresistible needed seeing. He found a large hotel, checked in. He was excited, and the thought of going to his room alone depressed him. He didn't want to sleep—he especially didn't want to have the dream again. Of late he'd been having it nightly, the self-twisting nightmare. So he wandered the lobby, taking in its smooth mauves and browns; he read menus in front of restaurants; he passed the bar by fast, then poked into a convention room. Rows of listeners, quiet. A bearded fellow up front, talking science. He heard the word "holocaust". He poked back out and read the sign: Convention of Physicians against Nuclear Proliferation. This seemed large enough for thought. He walked in, scanned and took a seat in the front row. A woman, maybe sixty years old, was taking the stage. She began to talk, but faltered in her first sentence. He liked what he saw in her eyes. She looked at him.

May squats in the sand, her limbs' grace unconsidered. I'd run off and returned with my pack, glad she'd said yes to a spontaneous picnic, and glad that, though my clothes were wadded tight in the pack, it would've been stranger to get dressed than stay not. I squat too, pulling fruit and bread out, and say, "Naked Lunch"—guessing she is literary and will laugh for me, and she does. We trade ordinary introductions, eat ordinary food, but this is no ordinary time. When she hears my name is Tucker she laughs as though it means something. She sits cross-legged facing me. A most revealing position. There it is then, May's thighs joining at an open point, the male notion of life's bull's-eye. My eyes fight to stray there; she smiles at this, so we both let them stray as they want. Her way is to smile constantly—but unlike syrupy types, whose faces strain with a habit smile, her smile renews itself always with fresh reasons. May finds cause to smile at everything: my ordinary words, her ordinary words, and, in the gaps, the sea and sky and occasional gull hovering over us, my sandwich in its eye. My sense of her climbs from the simply erotic. I see dustings of sand have adhered to the labial edges. A gritty-treasure mouth, an incongruence. I think of babies and broken glass, of garlic and sapphires in the mud. . . . May has the book beside her. Sometime during our talk she has covered over the title with a careful ridge of sand.

Behn was stunned at himself, horrified: he'd agreed and now he was following the big man to his apartment. How, why had he agreed? But something seemed fitting. He somehow remembered following him before—a *déjà vu*, he'd done this. The man was right—Behn did remember him. Especially in the room when he (the name, he recalled now, was Nathaniel) took off his coat to reveal the yellow T-shirt, too bright, too tight, a dark slice of hairy belly showing at the belt, which would've been beer-drinker macho had Nathaniel not been gay. Standing behind an art deco bar, a leaping ceramic horse at one end and a barber pole with clashing purple and mauve stripes at the other, Nathaniel poured two drinks. On the wall behind Nathaniel hung a wooden plaque, the kind that should have fronted a country driveway and said The Macleods'. This one said, Sex and Fear. The drinks he poured were fancy ones, eased in triple-layered with a spoon. Behn sat on the couch, still afraid, still feeling vulnerable, still like a woman who hadn't been put upon quite enough to run. Nathaniel approached with the drinks. The glasses they'd been poured in had magically changed to coffee mugs, and Behn's fear grew for not being able to see what he would be drinking. He took the cup, as he knew he would. Nathaniel sat down, not beside him, but across. Behn was surprised by his disappointment at this. Absurdly, he smiled a timid, seductive smile. He knew exactly what Nathaniel was going to say next.

So Dr. Helen Smol began talking to (or, in her mind, with) the red-eyed man in the front row. She could see he understood her. She could see he understood . . . this. The size of it. The concurrent smallness and vastness. The utter equivalence of any given detail and the universe which contained it. And he would understand the only equation worth considering: life and death and the difference between the two. She knew they would agree later, tomorrow perhaps, in her room, that there was no difference. He looked too young to have realized. It had taken her sixty years. The how and where of death didn't matter nearly so much as the what of it. Her next sentence was, "All of this has taken me sixty years to know. How old are you?" While the rest of the audience paused and thought, thinking this a rhetorical question, the man in the front row, who had by now forgotten his wife, her slap, his flight and his hangover, mouthed the word, forty-two.

TWISTS. After eating we settle back on the sand into a wordlessness. I feel uncomfortable but try to hide it. Something is about to happen. A step will be taken, either a goodbye or a step closer, and both scare me. I lie back and close my eyes. "Tucker," she says, after a time. She says my name slowly, chewing it, weighing. I grunt and smile and keep my eyes closed, feigning ease. "What do you think of your father?" she asks me. She too has fallen back, and she puts a hand on my arm, on my biceps, with her fingers just slightly into my armpit, almost erotic. In any case an intimacy. "I never knew him," I tell her. With her hand so, I will tell her anything. "I know that," she says. "What do think of him?" she repeats. I tell her I think of him as a gap. Something just not there. So vividly not there I experience him as almost solid. May is laughing now and I'm amazed. But she's squeezing my arm. "I'm here on purpose," she says. "Look." I go up on my elbows and she rearranges herself cross-legged. The book she places on the foot of ground between her heels and her vagina. May points to the authors' names. One is my father. "And this was my grandmother," she says, and puts a finger beside the name Helen Smol. "They're both dead," says May. The book's title is still covered with sand.

She finished speaking. Jack went to his room for the sole reason of using the phone. He sat on the bed, feeling with his ass the croak of over-clean sheets grating on each other. He saw the painting on the wall was tasteful, and signed. This room would be expensive. So would his family. How did one abandon a wife and son? In the face of the big questions—put to him tonight pissing in a boyhood bar, then again in a convention hall, from the mouth of an old woman he didn't know—did details such as morality matter? Could such small things as guilt survive the size of such a view? Poor little Tucker, they'd say. Yet in the grand equation their three lives were of no more import than three pencil dots on a pad, than three raindrops fallen to earth somewhere behind a nameless hill in Oregon. . . . Jack smiled at this. Then he wept, from the heart. It felt like his abdomen was swelling out and breaking apart. He wasn't so much saddened by this turn his life had taken as he was at the recognition that such sadness was a part of everyone's life, such sadness was part of the equation. He dialled. Her voice said a broken hello, she'd been asleep. "I'm leaving for good," he said, stressing the last word to give it double meaning. And before she could say anything: "I'll support you and Tucker. I'll never have sex again. But I've met someone." He added this last bit thinking of the murmurs he'd heard as he left the convention hall, after Dr. Smol had finished her speech by looking directly at him and saying, "My room number is four-eleven."

When Nathaniel handed him the drink, Behn heard himself say thank you exactly as a woman would. Nathaniel's little smile seemed worldly and tired, even bored, as though he'd been hoping for more challenge, for more hairy obstacles to conquest. In the impasse, Behn began to sweat. God, what was he doing? Who was he in fact? He thought of his friends, arm-punching football fans; he thought of all the girlfriends he'd had. And he had a son. Didn't he? And a wife? Or had he left them? Now, after glancing briefly at Nathaniel, he found himself scanning the apartment, smiling coyly at the pastel knicks and gaudy knacks he assumed typical of a homosexual lair. He watched himself stretch on the couch like a cat, a cat inviting a hand to its flanks. He was horny, good god, and he was sweating and afraid and disgusted. "Who..., " he began, even as he noticed his shirt was now something sheer, and a kind of mauve, and that he had breasts, breasts never touched by a hand. "Who are we?"

Helen Smol sat in her chair sipping room-service tea, her third pot this night. Having to pee again, she considered the complications of continuing to have a body. It seemed a rather arbitrary thing, but one that did have its beauty, that of a painful clockwork. A wedge of sunlight was splitting the curtain. She thought: my, ninety-three million miles, and there it is. And there was Jack, stirring on the bed, twisting, a moan. Where did nightmares fit? She and Jack had started well together, she dictating, he writing. His questions were reasonable, guided by his desire that this work communicate to people. His understanding was harmonious to hers, though incomplete. Words, quibbles, were his realm. And this, apparently, was why they had come together: one completing the other, two halves of the Aristotelian bean seed; one male, one female; the stasis of magnets hovering apart. She smiled: there was young Jack veritably convulsing on the bed. On her way to pee, she laid her hand on Jack's shoulder. She watched his eyes open and become aware of her before she moved on to the bathroom and sat down. His youth would help. Though her mind's direction was the essence of vitality, of greenness, it would suck more quickly the reservoir of her body, already old. How long would they live? And where would her mind take them? She leaned back, closed her eyes, laughed softly.

RESOLUTIONS. Even as Behn asked, Who are we? he began to know. A voice said, "We're a dream," but Behn didn't know who said it. He was no longer Behn in fact. All was convoluting quickly, each second more dreamlike now that the secret was out. Who was he? He was Jack, dreaming, but he was Behn as well. He was now watching himself through Nathaniel's eyes, and Nathaniel had become Nate, a construction foreman, thinner, hawkish, heterosexual and disgusted with this poof named Behn on the couch. Nate sneered, "Behn with a fucking 'H'?" Behn asked him, in effect asking himself, "You're not going to tell my friends? or my wife? or god not Tucker?" Now he was naked, on the couch, caught in a position of lounging that had been intended as seduction. Nate rolled his eyes at him and wolfed his drink in a manly way. Behn groped for cushions to cover himself. He knew it was a dream, he could even mouth a silent I-am-Jack-sleeping, but this didn't matter: shame tore at him with teeth sharper than possible awake. His body was a frail thing, weaker than tissue. He watched it drain of colour, grow transparent to the bones. His penis was bent and tiny, smaller than a snail, bait now for nothing. It grew greyer as he watched it, and began to smell of neglect. Now, ending as in so many dreams before, he was on the hard floor of a sordid, furnitureless room, wedged against the wall amid dust balls and dead-dry bugs, his breathing getting weaker, the choking soon to come—he hated this part—with Nate, who was now Tucker, his son, grown up and beautiful, standing over him, proclaiming as always in tones so resonant, "You are wasting *time*." Now the choking began. Death again.

Then, as always, Jack woke up. This time with a hand on his shoulder, not his wife's. Somehow, from its feel, he knew he would not have the dream again. Jack rose, stretched and took the coffee she handed him. He didn't feel at all shy. He went to wash his face, then came back to the paper and pencil, picking up from last night. She was ending the introduction now, and he wrote: "This is about how things fit into the whole. Looked at closely, a grain of sand shows us what a beach is. Looking wide, a beach shows us what sand can do. While this example is conceptual, this book's intention is only practical. Its manner is neither apologetic nor humble. There is no room for that." She paused between sentences, to let his hand catch up. She gazed gently. She didn't appear to be thinking. When he was ready, she spoke. "The beach is impossible without the grain of sand. In life, we can find purpose only in the tiny. 'Life' is in fact impossible without putting bits of food into your mouth, and taking one breath after another." Writing, Jack realized he didn't know where Helen lived, nor she him. Helen went off to the bathroom again. She was drinking countless cups of water. Jack flipped to the first page to reread the dedication to Tucker and someone named May, which had convinced him early that Helen Smol's mind was worth joining: "Perspective is knowledge. Knowledge is energy. Energy is immortal. The passing of energy is immortality. The knowledge of this is perspective." Helen returned. She fixed her robe over her legs and set her feet squarely on the floor. Her slippers, Jack thought, with their puffs and ribbons, made Dr. Smol look very old but entirely honest. She spoke. "There is only seeing and doing of small things, doing with care, seeing that each is the only event possible. Pick your lint with patience, and love." Jack, writing, said to her, "That's enough to make me scream." Helen dictated, "That might be enough to make one scream. But scream with heart." She looked at him. "And with humour." She looked at him, such an old lady. "And with respect."

She felt her death coming, though it might be months or years. This last part of life felt like being in bed late at night and having a burst of best clarity before going to sleep. She would live as long as she stayed awake. She would savour her widening mind, which meant savouring each rich sip of water, each word spoken, each body ache which explained to her the quality of existence. She told Jack, "Laughter is joy if seen while done." Where should they live? Somewhere small, and isolated, so they could avoid the coming randomness. The violent gathering. The summing. With a gesture Helen told Jack his pencil could stop, and she told him about his dream. She told him that just as he had woken up from that dream, so would he one day wake up from this one. Jack paused, then asked, "Well, who in hell is dreaming now?" Helen took a breath to speak, savouring it as she did. But she didn't answer him. Maybe there would be a chapter for it, should they be given time.

Watching me, May teases the sand off the title, inch by slow inch. "The. . . ." She's laughing. She wants me to enjoy this too. " . . . Summing. . . ." I'm thinking of my faceless father. " . . . of the. . . ." I watch her vagina too, flicking back and forth to it, and this is absurd. " . . . Parts." I look at her and smile and shrug, and she shrugs too. Neither of us knows where to go from here. I feel an erection coming, and feel silly for it, at such a time. But my awareness of it stops its rise, though an erection would be the most honest thing I could communicate to May at this moment. She hands me the book and I read some. I close it after a little. I am less excited now. It sounds true enough, but ordinary. But I like the dedication very much. Looking at May, I ask her, "Have you read this?" and she says she has. I nibble a cracker, feeling it snap at my lips and then mush up with saliva. I feel how important May and this cracker are, both. I look at her breasts. Reservoirs of some kind of continuity. At the same time they make me want to stroke her and moan and scream. They make me want to paint their careful picture; they make me want to bellow like an animal. I know at the core of things there is no contradiction in these extremes. "Maybe," I say, "it'll be fun to talk about this book, after I read it." But May knows my mind now, or maybe it is the way I've put the book down, quite far from me. "Maybe," she says, "we don't have to. Maybe it's old. We've been forced to learn a lot. After all that's happened." It is now two hours after daybreak, and soon the sun will be fatal. We have to get back. I notice the gulls have left already. Her place, she says, pointing, is that way. So she invites me. "I can borrow a partition for today, because they'll know it's special." I am grateful she has released me from the role of being the forward one. Yes, we are special. What does she know about me? There are no surprises for people any more. All we can do is feel bad or good about what takes place. We begin walking down the beach, quickly because the sun is rising whiter and whiter. I see on her back she's been blistered once, and death may be ticking away under her skin. May says, coming closer, "But there's a part of the book you'll love. Not all reading is a waste of time." Her voice is low and liquid, and I can picture it harmonizing atoms of air on the way to my ear, and past my head, and on and on into the particulate vista. "It tells us," she says, "what it will be like to wake up from this dream."